SOME FINAL BEAUTY AND OTHER STORIES

I0891650

The New Oeste Series

León Salvatierra and Daniel A. Olivas, *Series Editors*

The New Oeste series celebrates the outpouring of creative expression by Latinx writers in the American West of the twenty-first century. In border-breaking literary arts informed by perspectives as distinctive as the American West, the authors in the series explore the artistic, cultural, and intellectual connections between the region's complicated past and its diverse future. With a commitment to the power of prose and poetry to unite, educate, and enrich, the series editors seek to support projects from unique voices that invite connection and inclusion within the American West. Currently, the editors seek fiction, poetry, and creative nonfiction that expand conceptions of the West and its people.

Preparatory Notes for Future Masterpieces: A Novel
Maceo Montoya

The World Doesn't Work That Way, but It Could
Yxta Maya Murray

How to Date a Flying Mexican: New and Collected Stories
Daniel A. Olivas

To the North/Al norte: Poems
León Salvatierra

A History of Hazardous Objects: A Novel
Yxta Maya Murray

My Chicano Heart: New and Collected Stories of Love and Other Transgressions
Daniel A. Olivas

Some Final Beauty and Other Stories
Lisa Alvarez

Where Heaven Sinks: Poems
Maria Esquinca

Praise for *Some Final Beauty and Other Stories*

"Lisa Alvarez is a writer with a deep vision of the human possibilities and the moral questions of our time, and this luminous and empathic collection will reveal her to readers as a hidden gem of the West."

—Héctor Tobar, author of *Our Migrant Souls* and *The Barbarian Nurseries*

"Lisa Alvarez writes experienced protagonists. In *Some Final Beauty and Other Stories*, they navigate evolving relationships with parents, neighbors, and lovers; times of political upheaval; and the sharp demands of life with the knowledge and skills they've earned. Their stories are told in crystal clear prose that often opens into vivid, descriptive flourishes. Alvarez writes with the openness of a poet and the curiosity of every excellent fiction writer. Her stories are made real by this, as are her characters. Alvarez understands that experience does not mean that you stop seeking."

—Gustavo Hernandez, author of *Flower Grand First*

"These California stories are not city and not country but are in the cracks of the two colliding. Characters aren't living in the newest suburbs but older tract housing and apartment complexes, and Lisa Alvarez, with flowers in her hair, listens, tossing seeds."

—Dagoberto Gilb, author of *New Testaments: Stories*

"Lisa Alvarez's Southern California is one of melancholy and beauty, cities and canyons, insurrections and mariachis and secrets kept and spoken. Gorgeous pacing, storytelling prose—gorgeous."

—Gustavo Arellano, *LA Times* columnist and coauthor of *A People's Guide to Orange County*

"Lisa Alvarez's *Some Final Beauty and Other Stories* is a subtle counterpunch to the brutality, racism, cruelty, and injustice of an America emboldened by Ronald Reagan and Donald Trump alike. With balanced prose, an eye for details, and a wide-ranging perspective, Alvarez's stories are perceptive, graceful, entertaining, and insightful. Often marginalized, discounted, and ignored, Alvarez's characters are tactical and keen observers, and they have the blessing and curse of foresight. Regardless of the David and Goliath obstacles, their survival comes from right actions, and they thrive in quietly beautiful and profound ways. 'I am still a person who joins the march,' one explains, 'puts one foot in front of the other, who still believes in the words she chants, who carries signs lettered with impossible demands.' This is an essential story collection for this moment, one that offers hope and fortitude."

—Victoria Patterson, author of *The Secret Habit of Sorrow: Stories*

Some Final Beauty
and Other Stories

LISA ALVAREZ

UNIVERSITY OF NEVADA PRESS | *Reno & Las Vegas*

University of Nevada Press | Reno, Nevada 89557 USA

www.unpress.nevada.edu

Copyright © 2025 by Lisa Alvarez

All rights reserved

Manufactured in the United States of America

First Printing

Cover design by Michele Quinn
Cover illustration: *Woe Is Me to See What I Have Seen See What I See* by Andrea Bowers

Library of Congress Cataloging-in-Publication Data available upon request.

ISBN 978-1-64779-197-1 (paper)
ISBN 978-1-64779-198-8 (ebook)
LCCN: 2025003880

The paper used in this book meets the requirements of American National Standard for Information Sciences—Permanence of Paper for Printed Library Materials, ANSI/NISO Z39.48-1992 (R2002).

For Andrew

A friend asks, "What was at stake for you in the Eighties?" . . . Oliver North held up his right hand. Reagan turned off his hearing aid. Sentences fell apart but they had always been a part. Yeltsin. Walesa. Wall comes down. Romania. El Salvador. Noriega. Some elderly folk lived on dog-food when their pensions collapsed. People worried about children, lovers, ex-husbands, jobs. Consciousness stayed alive. Interest rates leapt through the vault of the sky. We cried & cried. We made food & quit smoking. We learned the names of wildflowers & forgot them & relearned them. This was only the beginning. There's so much more to be said in answer to your question.

—Brenda Hillman, "The Eighties"

I was right to invent for my friends and our children a report on these private deaths and the conditions of our lifelong attachments.

—Grace Paley, "Friends"

Contents

SOME FINAL BEAUTY AND OTHER STORIES

Everyone Was Singing "Freiheit"

The bus was running late, so Laurie arrived just after the memorial service began. Because every folding chair in the church's community room was filled, she stood next to Max and Annette, an elderly couple she knew from evenings spent stuffing envelopes. Laurie suspected that she had folded and unfolded each of those chairs several times over during the course of weekly meetings and other events throughout the last year. She knew well the cool weight of the cream-colored metal, the familiar creaking resistance, and then the satisfying snap-into-place. The placard on the wall announced that the room seated one hundred. At least two dozen more people stood. Cracks were still visible in the drywall from the recent earthquake.

Everyone was singing "Freiheit." A cheerful chubby banjo-playing man led them, translating each verse in carefully enunciated English before returning to the original German. Some looked down at the lyrics, extra large on half sheets of paper. But most, like Max and Annette, didn't have to. They marched through these verses, singing in robustly gruff-sounding syllables about the Spanish heavens and plains, the far-off homeland and the fascists, the bullets falling like hail and their comrades in the trenches.

As soon as the song was finished, Annette turned to Laurie. "I haven't sung 'Freiheit' in years," she said. Her large eyes, brown and rimmed with black eyeliner, were wet. She pulled a tissue from her purse. It was an old-lady purse, a grandmother's purse, well stocked, Laurie thought, ready for anything. She spied a pack of gum, individually wrapped peppermint pinwheel mints, a fat wallet, a stash of ballpoints and the red makeup pencil Annette would need to repair the damage to her crying eyes.

The memorial was for Herman Rosenberg, who had sung "Freiheit" decades earlier as a member of the Abraham Lincoln Brigade, that assembly of anti-fascists who had gone to fight Franco. His son took the podium to deliver the eulogy, pointing to the enlarged photo of his father as a young man, posing with his fellow soldiers and an American flag.

"Premature anti-fascists," the son said. "The war before the good war."

The mourners were aging *brigadistas* and *internationalistas* as well as survivors of other battles, like Max, whose tattoo, numbers stained blue, was visible on one forearm when he rolled up his sleeves. The first time they met, Max had advised Laurie that, in his opinion, everyone needed to belong to a brigade or liberation front at least once. Max offered loads of advice.

That night, almost a year earlier, the volunteer crew had to prepare a fundraising appeal for bulk mailing: folding letters, stuffing envelopes, sealing, stamping, and addressing. A full evening's work. After watching Laurie fold and refold the appeal letter, Max pointed out the space between paragraphs that she could use as a natural measure. It was right below the sentence *If we don't speak out for El Salvador, for Elba Ramos, her daughter, and the six Jesuit priests, who will?*

"This one's yours, I guess, isn't it? Your liberation front. Everyone needs one." Max nodded toward the emblem printed on the letterhead: a dove with an olive branch in its beak flew over a map of a tiny country shaped like a shoe. El Salvador. In his voice, she could hear what her maternal grandmother might call "the old country." Her grandmother's old country, the one her parents had come from, no longer existed.

Laurie did not want to confess that this liberation front was not hers, nor this church, that she didn't belong to anything or anyone—she was here only to perform community service, a deal with a judge and attorneys and the DA, an impossible number of hours to be served. This was the consequence of poor choices involving alcohol and drugs, and even poorer choices involving a car she could no longer drive even if it could be driven, even if it was hers. It was why she took the bus. Or walked. Resided in a so-called halfway house that was exactly halfway between the church and her old high school. Showed up for the church AA meetings and unfolded the chairs and set up the coffee urns. Two regular, one decaf. Lots of sugar. Then she stayed to fold up the chairs afterward and pour what was left of the hot coffee in the gutter, watching it steam into the night as it ran down the appropriately named Hill Street. This was why she folded the endless appeal letters in thirds without complaint and moistened the glue on the envelopes. She didn't read them. Didn't think twice about the dove. Didn't really want to think.

Despite his age, Max still had muscular forearms, deeply tanned. Popeye's arms without the anchors. It wasn't too hard to see the tattooed numerals on one forearm: old, crude, half hidden in the thinning thicket of the gray hair there. Her own tattoos crawled up her pale skinny arms and shoulders, danced across her back and down her legs, an incoherent circus. Tiger. Monkey. Lion. Peacock. Camel. Seal. A murder of crows. A smiling dolphin swimming under a rainbow. An impulse-driven dragon that a cute guy had talked her into getting on the boardwalk one summer. He'd gotten one too and, for a time, they were a couple, a couple with twin dragons flying on their biceps. But that was over now too. She had to get her act together. She was twenty-five.

Annette admired them all, as if Laurie had drawn the tattoos herself. "Which one was first, dear?" she'd asked that night, a year ago, when they were still strangers.

Laurie pointed to her right ankle, exposed in a flat sandal. Hello Kitty, fat-headed, pink-bowed, mindless, and friendly. Fat paw waving.

"Ooooh," Annette responded. "Adorable."

Was Annette serious? Her own grandmother winced whenever she caught sight of any of her tattoos, even the benign kitty. And her mother had told her she just pretended her daughter's menagerie was temporary and would one day disappear. Her father, the psychologist, who had left when she was a child, congratulated her dryly on finding the one thing that would drive her mother crazy forever. "The permanence is what's truly brilliant," he said. "I wish I had thought of it." Laurie retorted that her tattoos were not about her mother, but her father just gave her that look. "It's always about our mothers, dear," he said.

"Do you *really* like them?" she asked. She felt like she could ask Annette anything. After all, no one really knew who Laurie was. And she didn't know who any of them were either, even though it was clear to her that they knew each other, or at least each other's type. Laurie's days and evenings were now spent with these two groups: upstairs the do-gooders, like Annette and Max, most old but a few young, trying, it was becoming clear to her, to save the world, or at least a part of the world, and then downstairs the AA and the NA and the ACA and the Al-Anon folks trying to save themselves. So many acronyms and abbreviations. So much urgency and desperation, upstairs and down. Downstairs the emphasis was on the power they didn't have. Upstairs it was all about the power they wanted. Those letters all asking versions of that same question: *If we don't speak out for El Salvador, for Elba Ramos, her daughter, and the six Jesuit priests, who will?* That night, Laurie folded the sheet of paper so the bottom matched up to that line. Five hundred times. What was interesting was that these upstairs people instantly presumed Laurie was one of them, that she belonged. That she cared about Elba Ramos and her daughter and the priests. Her father would be fascinated.

"Oh, yes, dear. Tattoos are such a statement. It is *art,* isn't it? So personal. It's what *you* care about. But tell me, why the cat? Why the little fat cat with the hair bow?" Annette asked as if it mattered. Those brown eyes of hers, full of curiosity, even at her age. So sincere that it was almost embarrassing. Everything mattered to this little old lady. Everything.

Laurie shrugged. "Hello Kitty was my favorite when I was a kid. I could never get enough. My parents thought she was cheap. Now I have her forever." Laurie remembered the wanting, that juvenile desire for what everyone else had, and her mother's words: "You don't want *that,* dear," delivered with a little sniff. But Laurie did want that. She wanted that cheap friendly cat.

Annette nodded, satisfied. "Good for you," she said. She looked down at the diminishing stack of letters. "You're going to need some more."

Laurie looked around for the minister who signed her timesheet. Everyone referred to him as Jim. She couldn't do that, even though he had gently corrected her when she called him Father. Now she just called him sir or Minister Jim. He was also mayor of this sleepy coastal city. This had been news to her, even though she'd lived here all her life. It perhaps explained why she had been assigned here, to this church. No doubt it was a favor for her parents—who, she had begun to appreciate since the accident, were people of some social standing, of some power. Dad, the shrink; Mom, the restaurateur, her upscale eatery showcasing dishes from Laurie's grandparents' disappeared country of origin. A deal must have been struck. Minister Jim usually supervised the assembly line on the collapsible card tables: folders, stuffers, labelers, closers, and stampers; troubleshooting and anticipating needs for more envelopes or labels; sometimes kneeling in front of the cantankerous copy machine to extract a stubborn misfeed or refill the paper supply. Occasionally he played pinball on the Dolly Parton–themed machine that stood like an improbable altar in between a tall bookcase filled with old hymnals and a squat metal file cabinet.

The pinball machine was a great mystery to Laurie. How had it been carried up the church's narrow interior stairway? She wondered about the place of such a thing in a minister's office. Of course, there was the wonder of Dolly herself, with her trademark blond voluptuousness, resplendent in a revealing yellow pantsuit. When the machine was on, when the tokens dropped into the slot, the singer glowed. Laurie hoped Dolly would sing, but it was just a game, a single silver ball triggering buzzers and bells and lights. Pinball Dolly was lush and blank, and when Laurie played, as she did at least once almost every day—it was free, after all—she saw her own faint reflection superimposed on the singer: slender, dark drippy hair, pale skin adorned with scrambling inky beasts.

"I'm glad you could make it to Herman's service, dear," Annette remarked when the service was over. "He liked you so, you know," she said. "You reminded him of his Millie. The way you laughed at his terrible jokes."

Laurie didn't have the heart to tell Annette that she was still on the clock, following orders, here not for Herman but to serve her required hours. After cleanup, she'd bring her timesheet to Minister Jim and have him sign off, another three hours subtracted from what she owed the state.

⚜

The school bus Laurie had T-boned had been empty except for the bus driver, who looked like he'd seen his fair share of drunk drivers and accidents. The last of the students he'd dropped off saw the whole thing, standing on the corner of Hollister and Fourth. They were witnesses, not that more witnesses were needed. It had happened in broad daylight, as people said on such occasions, when that's all you could say about such obvious public stupidity. Onlookers at the corner liquor store and the pocket park were more than enough to prove that the car had slammed into the school bus without so much as braking, and then ricocheted into the boundary wall. Laurie was lucky, the bus driver told her, even before the paramedics arrived to extract her from her vehicle with the jaws of life. But Laurie didn't feel lucky. The car (not hers) was totaled. She was holding. She was under the influence. For some time after, she could make out the sinister streaks on the cinderblock wall into which somehow, after hitting the bus, the car had slammed, skidded, and come to rest. She thought of it as the shadow of the accident, as if the event had cast its own mark through speed and scratch and heat. Then one day it was painted over, just like that.

Gone. Forgotten. Or maybe forgiven, Laurie hoped.

⚜

This is how Laurie saw it: she had so many hours of community service. Too many! And she had those Twelve Steps to climb.

Both could be achieved in the same place, the Methodist church on Hill Street. Here she was, upstairs or down, nearly every day and night of the week. How much longer could this go on? When she wasn't stuffing envelopes upstairs with people who could be her grandparents—if her grandparents had been aging commies and leftists and old hippies, which they most certainly were not—she was downstairs in a dreary circle with the AA crowd and the NA crew, listening to their stories and sharing her own, which always ended with the yellow school bus and her friend's father's Mustang and that cinderblock wall. The bump of the curb, the crack of the axle, the shearing of the tires.

Five months earlier, her sponsor, Ivette, had begun to gently press Laurie to share more, intercepting her as she set up the coffee and unpacked the enormous blue tin of Danish sugar cookies, stacked in their crinkled paper cups, as yellow and swirly as Pinball Dolly. "Tonight tell us more. Not just the story that brought you here. If you're anything like most of us, and you are, you know you are, you have other stories, stories you need to tell. It will help."

Laurie looked at her. Ivette came to the church dressed up and wearing lipstick, as if going to a meeting was a big deal. Laurie knew all about her because Ivette had laid it all out: the three kids taken from her, the kids who, even as adults, wouldn't speak to her. The broken marriage. Something about cashing in her daughter's U.S. savings bonds for drugs. A very, very bad boyfriend. But for Laurie wasn't the car, the bus, the wall enough? She knew how to tell that story. It did the job.

She looked around. The early arrivals were filing in before the coffee had even begun to perk. Some waited outside, smoking. What else could she offer up? At the time of the accident, she'd had cocaine in a tiny aluminum foil envelope tucked inside her sock. A quarter gram. She got away with it somehow, trapped in the car, peeling off shoes and socks using only her toes so she could emerge barefoot. How about the high school English teacher who, instead of busting her for the stash in her reading folder, confiscated her kit and didn't say a word? Mr. Morrison. She saw him suddenly, still behind his desk, his carefully tended afro backlit by the afternoon sun through the classroom window, watching her discover what was gone. Two months from graduation. Was he trying to save her? Or did he just not want the hassle? Or did he want the stash for himself? The matches, the foil, the straw, the crumbly brown powder. She never knew. She graduated, walked across that stage. Mr. Morrison shook her hand, wished her well. Most of her stories were about getting away with it. But you weren't supposed to share stories in AA that didn't feature your regret. Laurie knew that much.

"I'll try," she said to Ivette. But she didn't mean it. And that night, she told her story as she always had.

Getting away with things was a hard habit to break. Laurie was good at it, and it had worked for her so far. Minister Jim pointed this out one night as she waited for him to finish her weekly paperwork. He took his time. The previous week he had caught her trying to double-dip, a term she'd previously applied only to ice cream cones bought at the pier. He accused her of attempting the miracle of bilocation, which only five Catholic saints had ever demonstrated, and then proceeded to tell her about all five. The stories of being in two places at once were surprisingly boring. If she could be in two places at once, she would make better choices than those saints. Minister Jim's favorite was Isidore, the patron saint of farmworkers, who had appeared in the field working the harvest at the same time he was seen in church praying.

Laurie hadn't thought Minister Jim would notice that she had claimed to be in Twelve Step meetings at the same time she was also upstairs with Max and Annette and the premature anti-fascist battalion stuffing envelopes for justice. So she sat in his tiny office while he examined her entries and tallied up hours and meanwhile made her talk. He was good at that.

Minister Jim's office was like his pinball machine. Unexpected. He could have chosen the larger space on the second floor with the big windows, but instead he allowed the local peace and justice organizations to work there. His office looked like a storage closet, but it was large enough for what he needed: a desk, a bookcase, a few chairs. Spare. Monastic. The wood-paneled walls made it warm instead of oppressive. He made it warm too. Even when he was scolding, as he did that night—firm, hurt, disappointed—his round, suntanned face beamed hope. He was a man of faith, after all. Laurie sat and waited. She had no choice.

"But I don't understand what you have to get away with," he was saying. He had finished signing the forms but had placed them on his desk and folded his hands on top.

"This is where you tell me that I had everything growing up? That I still do?"

He waited. When he smiled, his face grew rounder, sun-like. Ivette had told her that Minister Jim was a surfer. That he took the short walk with his board from the rectory to the waves at least twice a week. This explained the tan, the sun-bleached, albeit thinning, hair, and the laidback attitude, but Laurie thought it was too much. Minister? Mayor? Surfer? How many things could one person be? She suspected Ivette nurtured a secret crush on him.

"You should talk to my parents. You're going to, aren't you? You know my parents, don't you?" She heard her voice. A petulant whine, like she was a kid who wanted Hello Kitty. She was embarrassed. Where did that come from? She was twenty-five years old.

Jim sighed, a bit theatrically, or maybe he was just tired. "This isn't about your parents," he told her. "This is about you. My relationship here is with you. And it's not about the numbers." He looked down at the papers, then back at her. "It's about what the time here is doing for you."

"I am doing everything I'm told," she said steadily. The bare walls of the office were now bothering her. There was nothing to look at. Maybe that's why he kept it like this. She arched her ankle and looked down. Hello Kitty waved. Mute.

"Yes, except for your adventures with bilocation, you are doing everything you are told. But you're still trying to get away with it, aren't you? Instead of getting *with it*. You're just doing what you've always done."

"I'm sober," she responded. "I am clean. Two months."

"Because they test you," he said evenly. "You pee into a cup while someone waits outside the door and listens. You can't get away with anything there, not yet. But this?" He pointed at the paper again. "My church. My word."

Laurie tried to imagine him in the water, black neoprene suit and surfboard, the object of Ivette's sober ecumenical desires. Minister Jim possessed the kind of confident patience required to wait out natural forces, to read the waves. He was, she thought, trying to read her also. Maybe she too was a wave.

"I hear you surf," she said.

"I do," he said. "For fun." He was smiling again, just like that. "What do you do for fun?"

Her silence was longer and deeper than she intended or he expected. Lying would have been quicker. It always was. "Your pinball machine," she said finally. "The Dolly Parton. That's fun."

"I agree," he said. He was pleased. "Anything else?"

She was thinking now, hard. "I like pouring out the hot coffee in the street after meeting," she admitted.

This seemed to impress him. "Anything else?"

She thought some more. "Stuffing envelopes isn't exactly fun, but the people aren't bad," she said. "I think they think I'm fun. Does that count?"

"We'll count that," he said, assuming an officious tone. He picked up his pen and made an entry on some imaginary tally sheet in the air. "Please note that Laurie herself is fun."

She remembered Annette's interest in her tattoos, Herman's pleasure in having made her laugh at his corny jokes. This was getting easier. "Herman's fun."

"Herman Rosenberg is indeed fun," Minister Jim pronounced. "Most everyone is in agreement on this." He added another entry on the pretend tally sheet.

"Can I go now?" she asked. "It will not be fun if I miss my bus."

"You may," he said, handing over the papers. "Have fun."

It was a busy Wednesday night, some weeks after Laurie had been busted for bilocation. Minister Jim was downtown, heading up a special city task force meeting on homelessness. "I'm putting you in charge," he joked as he left. Laurie knew he'd be back to lock up, but she liked that he joked with her. Al-Anon was downstairs, and upstairs the SANE/Freeze monthly membership mailer was in the works. This mailing came with a special refrigerator magnet featuring Mahatma Gandhi reclining next to a surfboard. "Wipeout War," it read. This meant each envelope required an extra stamp. One more step in the assembly-line process. Annette and Max were folding and stuffing, and Herman and Laurie had been sealing and stamping. That evening, Herman told a story Laurie had not heard before. It was about his mother, who hadn't wanted him to fight in Spain and so had hidden his passport. Herman got another one, applying under his mother's maiden name. "I showed her," he said, cackling. "I showed the government too."

Usually Laurie just listened but this night she was thinking. Maybe it was the magnetic Gandhi and its slogan that made her think to question him. She waited until Herman's youthful ingenuity had been admired and his mother's rightful concern acknowledged but then she observed: "But here you are, working for a peace group. How does that work?" She really wanted to know.

"I was working for peace then too," Herman said. "Trying to stop a bigger war."

"Did you?" she asked. "Stop a bigger war?" As soon as she said it, she realized she didn't know what she was asking, that she might have gone too far.

Everyone was quiet. Max and Herman exchanged looks. Annette kept folding the letters. They heard voices from the meeting below. Someone was complaining loudly about their father. "I never had a real conversation with that bastard. Not one." Then quiet.

"Well, we did what we could," Herman said, his hearty Bronx accent softened to a sudden sad whisper as he slid a sealed envelope her way.

"That's all you can do against fascists," Annette added.

"Well, I can think of a few more things that could have been done," remarked Max.

"Always more to be done," said Herman. "Never enough. Look where we are now." He coughed.

"How old were you?" Laurie asked.

"So many questions!" Annette laughed, almost back to her loud self. "After all this time, she finally talks?"

Laurie blushed. There was applause from downstairs.

"Twenty-one," Herman said. "Younger than you. Imagine that."

"We were all in our twenties," said Annette. "Everyone was."

"That's impossible, my dear," said Max. "Everyone couldn't have been in their twenties."

"I know," replied Annette, "but that's what it felt like."

The good feeling returned. Soon they finished the first run and as they waited for the next stack from the printer, Laurie left the table and slid a token into Dolly, who brightened up right away.

At first Laurie imagined she had made the machine tilt with one too many bumps of her hip. She was juggling a multi-ball play, hoping to cradle the first ball with one flipper and use a roll shot with the other flipper to ricochet the second ball into a jackpot, which would trigger a cascade of bells and whistles and, she anticipated, another extra ball. Then she would just keep feeding them one by one into the jackpot. She hoped to catapult her score into the Top Ten, which was currently dominated by Minister Jim. She was close. But then, as the vibrations increased, Dolly dimmed. The flippers stilled and the lights went out. The tremors became sharper, stronger. People shouted downstairs but the roaring of the quaking earth was too loud, like a train had turned down Hill Street heading for the shore.

When it was over, the darkness in the two-story wood-framed church was total. Laurie, who had dropped to her knees and huddled under a table, followed Max's old-country voice as he directed them to the stairwell. "Crawl," he ordered, and she did. She heard Annette scrambling in front of her, and once they reached the first floor, she could see by the moonlight shining in the windows. Annette was dragging her purse, but she was barefoot. No doubt the sandals she always kicked off under the table were still upstairs. Laurie could hear the barking of dogs, a distant chorus of car alarms. The Al-Anon folks crowded around the anteroom as if eager to resume their meeting. "It isn't safe," Max declared, his voice unexpectedly bold in the darkness. She and everyone else followed him into the street.

Inside the old church, Laurie had feared the world outside had crumbled and that she might have to crawl to the halfway house through streets of rubble, but now that she was out in it, she could see that the world was beautifully intact. She could even hear the waves crashing at the beach. Distant sirens not unlike coyote howls. A sense of post-earthquake giddiness was already beginning to ripple through the people milling on Hill Street.

This would be one of *those* quakes, notable but not disastrous. Not like, say, Loma Prieta, which had happened last year, or the Sylmar quake of her childhood, which had sloshed the water from their backyard pool. This would be a respectable quake. Its modest casualties would mostly be flukes. Later, everyone would have their personal earthquake story. Hers would be the Dolly Parton pinball machine and the old lefties she shook, rattled, and rolled with before crawling after them on her knees. Her parents would like this story. Laurie pictured telling them at one of their rare family dinners, seated in a back booth of her mother's restaurant, a platter piled high with steaming pierogies in front of them.

When the earth rumbled again, someone shouted with a kind of glee: "Aftershock!"

"Stay out of the building!" Max shouted. "It is old. It is not safe."

Laurie saw Annette fishing Band-Aids from her purse and offering them to Ivette, who sat on the curb watching blood run down her long bare shin from a gash on her knee. Except for her wound, Ivette was, like the world, beautifully intact, high heels, pencil skirt, and all.

"Can I help?" Laurie asked.

"I think we're fine here, dear," said Annette. "But have you seen Herman?"

Laurie looked around and saw he was not where she would expect him to be, huddled with the smokers on the corner, listening to their stories. Herman was like that. He took an interest in people. Had he been in front of her as they scuttled down the stairs? Or had he been behind? Then she realized Herman hadn't been anywhere, that she had not heard his thick Bronx accent in the darkness or the aftermath. By now he should have been making jokes, wisecracks about the earthquake.

Max called her name as she ran back into the church, but Laurie didn't stop.

The earthquake would eventually have a name. As it turned out, it wasn't their earthquake after all but belonged to the desert, where casualties were high. Its official name came later, from an unfamiliar place, a dusty distant point of origin, a fault line previously unknown. Like the wars that didn't have names, not until the fighting was done and people finally figured out what was being fought for and why.

The earthquake didn't kill Herman, though he liked to claim it might have had not Laurie raced in after him. He was like that also. He elevated the tale he told of his rescue to epic status, casting Laurie as a fearless heroine. She found him pinned under the hymnal bookcase, ready with a joke about the fate of an atheist Jew stuck in a collapsing church. It wasn't a good joke, but he made the effort. No, it was those cigarettes that killed Herman, not long after the temblor, just as his wife Millie had always warned.

The day of his service, Laurie stayed late, sweeping up, pouring the leftover coffee down the gutter. Annette and Max offered to help, but she waved them off, watching as they made their way to the beach just in time for the sunset. She dumped the ice from the drink coolers into the planter beds, spreading it out gently with her hands. Herman, smoking on the corner, had once suggested this when he saw her poised to throw the contents of an ice bucket into the street. "Ice now, water later," he said. "Think about it. The plants will thank you."

She smirked then, but she didn't do so now. The crushed ice, melting into the parched soil, glittered. Her hands were cold, clean.

When it was time to go, she didn't climb the stairs to Minister Jim's office to get her paperwork signed even though she knew he was up there. She could hear the pinball machine: *Ding, ding, ding*. A jackpot. He would be expecting her. Let him, she thought. Instead, the community room restored to order, its chairs folded and stacked, Laurie turned the lights off and shut the doors behind her. She walked home in the warm summer night, the lyric sheet folded carefully in her pocket as if she might have future occasions to sing the song again.

A Pretty Penny

Robyn wouldn't wear secondhand shoes. Her feet, she said, were too tender. But me, my favorite shoes of all time remain a pair of old-school ice skates, made street wearable by prying off the ancient blades, thick, heavy as horseshoes. New red shoelaces, and I was ready to go anywhere. I pretended to skate sometimes, circling around a fire hydrant, gliding down the sidewalk and twirling into a bunny hop or a flip. It made Robyn laugh. I nailed the blades to the wall above our door for good luck. In the end, this cost me our $100 security deposit.

We were trying to live simply, as the bumper sticker on our door declared, so others might simply live.

Robyn's life was simpler because her parents sent her money.

I talked to mine as often as she did, a couple times a year, but hers lived thousands of miles away in London and mine lived in Lomita, which was the opposite of London. This was in 1984 and long-distance calls still cost, as my father would say, a pretty penny. I was living in Los Angeles with Robyn, twenty miles and three bus rides from my folks. My phone calls home didn't last long enough to cost much, often ending with my father hanging up, the heavy handset of his old rotary phone slamming into my ear, or else my mother whispering, "Not now, not now."

Our studio apartment was on the second floor of a four-story building so close to the 10 freeway we could hear its steady rumble—like the ocean, we bragged. Ours was the corner unit, a single room with two broad windows in a building built before we were born, with fire escapes climbing up its stucco sides like rusty vines.

We moved in on the day of Ronald Reagan's second inauguration, the coldest day on record in D.C. and one of the warmest ever in January in L.A. We wore white wife beater tank tops with no bras and green army pants cut off above the knee. When our long black hair grew too long, we gave each other trims and scattered the clippings from the windows for birds to use to feather their nests. Our new neighbors assumed we were lesbians. We thought we were, too. God knows I tried. Back then it seemed the only choice a rational woman could make—living in the patriarchal world, as it was. I had done my reading and arrived at this inescapable conclusion, this apartment, this woman.

We went to the Take Back the Night marches and Silence Equals Death rallies. We marched arm in arm with strangers we called sisters and brothers, and meant what we said. Later, there'd be a cheap curry plate at the Irish pub celebrating our victory in the streets, no matter how small the turnout or how indifferent or hostile the cops. Then we'd return home and collapse on our bed.

At first the futon mattress lay on the linoleum floor, wedged in the corner, the two windows above our de facto headboard. Later we placed it atop plastic milk crates scavenged from alleys, the warnings stamped in white letters: *Unauthorized use or possession of milk cases is against the law*. The crates were the color of children's alphabet blocks, bright primaries. We stored our clothes inside. We wore the same size, the same clothes. At night we'd lie in the dark and let the streetlights light up our bodies as we moved over, into, under each other.

Robyn was, she herself confided the first night we met, descended from an infamous early twentieth-century lesbian writer.

"What about you, June?" she asked. It was happy hour at Little Frida's. Margaritas for $1, the same for fish tacos. Free chips. In the patterned mirror behind the bar, we looked not unlike that famous Kahlo painting of the two Fridas, dark-haired but with faint glittering mustaches of salt.

Robyn's question was, I thought, a very British one, this concern about lineage, bloodlines. I didn't like the question, but I liked her.

"I'm descended from a Korean War vet and a Korean War orphan," I told her.

"So that's it," she said, squinting at me the way people do when they're trying to figure out what I am. They know I am something, but they don't know exactly what.

"That's it," I replied.

The infamous woman-loving writer's first and only novel was notorious for being banned—and later read like a sacred text by a generation of lesbians who styled themselves after the defiant writer, angularly mannish, yes, in that 1920s post-flapper fashion, but with cleavage and legs and a penchant for cloche hats. We, of course, owned a copy, a 25-cent paperback, discovered in the bountiful secondhand stacks of Wilshire Books. It joined our nightstand library, tucked between Adrienne Rich and Monique Wittig, *This Bridge Called My Back*, *Sisterhood Is Powerful*, and other canonical texts, each a bargain, purchased for no more than a buck. Other used bookstores featured cats or complimentary coffee, but Wilshire Books had the biggest women's studies section west of Sisterhood Books, plus a comely belly dancer, and so it earned our customer loyalty. The creamy blond daughter of the bearded bookstore owner often donned her flowing bejeweled dancing garb during business hours. As she walked the aisles, she jingle-jangled. While we browsed, we'd listen for the telltale tinkling swag of chains and coins at her slim ankles, followed the slivery finger bracelets as they disappeared up her sleeves while she rang up our purchases, and pretended to sigh as she shimmied back through the stacks.

"The author's my great-aunt," Robyn bragged to her the afternoon we brought the book, a slim volume.

"That so?" responded the bookstore belly dancer, who never seemed interested in any of the actual books, who, in fact, seemed profoundly bored by her role in the family business, and was unwilling to be engaged now, despite Robyn's overture. The cover of the infamous lesbian aunt's notorious book was stark, a black-and-white photo of three veiny leaves drying on the pavement.

I counted out the coins to drop into her palm: two dimes, one nickel.

She handed the book to us, a complimentary bookmark tucked inside, without further comment.

It sat on our shelf for weeks, untouched, until I read it in one sitting on a long afternoon, looking for the scandalous sex. The rest, I thought, was often impenetrable, a series of bleak and imagistic prose poems, outcasts wandering about from one degraded night to another. The sex was unimpressive, strange, subdued, buried in meandering nocturnal sentences. Nothing I didn't know. I expected, wanted, more.

"I am a cultural worker." That's what I would tell my father when he asked how I made a living. I had left college without a degree but with lots of ideas. "Cultural worker" was a term I learned in my Socialist study group, a circle of readers who met monthly in a downtown restaurant called Gorky's that never closed, where a bowl of borsht as red as the revolution cost you $1.50, a slice of dark rye bread a quarter. Sour cream was extra. My cultural work was my activism—the meetings I attended, the rallies, the marches, the books I read. I volunteered to raise money for good causes: a shoe factory in El Salvador, a women's health clinic in South Central, a Meals on Wheels–type program for people living with AIDS. I was full-time for the Revolution.

Meanwhile, my father worked behind the counter of a Gardena liquor store owned by a refugee, a man who came over on a boat from Vietnam. Dad, a mildly disabled Korean War veteran, sat behind that counter and rang up cheap booze day in, day out, and locked the day's take in a floor safe at night. He never understood how someone—not him—could be here for only a few years and own a business. "America's a great country," I remember him saying. I don't know if he believed it, but he'd say it from time to time, as if to remind himself. We'd be watching TV, detectives or doctors, comedy or mystery, me cross-legged on the living room rug, him in one recliner, my mother in the other, some kind of sewing in her lap. Or we'd be at the dining room table finishing dinner—peppered pork chops, mashed potatoes, applesauce, a frozen brick of green beans boiled in water—and he'd get my mother to describe once again how she'd come here after the war, sponsored by Lutheran World Relief. A girl, an orphan. "You see, June," he'd say to me, fork raised, "America's a great country. Don't you forget it."

When I was young and didn't know better, I used to ask him why, after the war was over, he didn't just bring my mother home with him. He had brought an ashtray made from a grenade and other souvenirs. Why did she have to wait so long? I didn't understand that they hadn't met in Korea, that my mother had been a child during the war, and later, when she came here, some might have called her a child bride, or a mail-order bride, or both.

Cultural work didn't pay the rent even though my share was, utilities included, $125. So I labored in a catering outfit, decorating fish-shaped salmon pâtés with olives and parsley, fluffing beds of butter lettuce to hold pink shrimp, split tails of glistening lobsters. I stacked tiny finger sandwiches filled with chicken and tuna salad. I carved roses out of tomatoes and tulips out of radishes. When I worked big parties, I stashed unopened bottles of Chardonnay deep in the garden ivy to be retrieved later. I carried the loot home in my backpack so Robyn and I could feast in our bed, food I'd never seen on my family's suburban dinner table: tinned smoked oysters, wheels of cheese in red wax, artichoke hearts, hard rolls, salami, those heavy-bottomed bottles of purloined wine.

Robyn would open the thin blue airmail envelopes filled with money orders that arrived monthly. "My cheques," she called them, and I imagined I could hear the "q-u-e-s" when she spoke the word in her clipped accent. Robyn. My Christopher Robin, I called her.

But then, suddenly, just like that, at the end of the decade, just as Reagan was leaving office, Robyn wanted to fix cities, repair the growing holes in the urban sprawl. Maybe it was the money her parents sent—or the money they threatened to stop sending. Maybe it was the changing view outside our windows: a multi-story studio complex went in with a fountain garden we could hear but not see, a rhythmic corporate challenge to the freeway's roar. Local efforts to block the development had failed despite petitions, protests, and sympathetic EIR reports. Besides, we were being priced out. It was time to move. So, Robyn went to UC Santa Barbara, two hours north, to study. Graduate school, she said. Urban planning. I joked that I conducted my own urban studies in a downtown loft.

I visited her once. It was beautiful, that big school by the ocean, the little student town with all the streets named after Spanish artists: Picasso, Cervantes, El Greco. Her room was twice the size of our old place and she shared it with no one. She covered the white walls with maps of Spanish cities: Madrid, Cordoba, Seville. Her new motto was pinned above her desk: "There is no new world you can make without the old world."—Jane Jacobs. Robyn's bed was large, a map of Toledo pinned above it. All those twisting streets, like a children's maze of a fairytale town. The castle at one end, the golden plaza at the center, the cathedral, the river winding around the ancient walls, the sudden dead ends, and the unexpected junctions.

"Why Toledo?" I asked.

"It's Anthony's favorite city," she said. She'd met Anthony at the university, a nice guy, she told me the one night we spent together in that large room. The son of vintners. They were studying the same thing, in the same field. "We're going to get married and it's where we'll go on our honeymoon." She held me. We were naked beneath the sheets, no longer pressed so firmly together but when she said this, she drew me to her again, just a little, and held me hard.

The wedding took place a bit further up the coast, at the family vineyard in Paso Robles. Golden dry hills rose above the rows and rows of grape vines that radiated out from the estate house. After the rehearsal dinner the night before, after tables of grand food that reminded me of those parties I once worked, the ones I stole from, I spent the night with Robyn, on the grounds in a remote cottage with trellised roses clambering up its sides. Very romantic. Anthony was very understanding, Robyn said. We dressed the next day, looking not unlike sisters in our simple dresses. I finally met Robyn's parents, who assured me that they had heard so much about me through the years, all good things. Robyn's elegant mother looked just like her daughter and her dead aunt, that famous lesbian writer—tall, rangy, all cheekbones and shins. Robyn often remarked that her mother was fond of saying that all women age into either goats or cows. Robyn and her mother, with their fine British bones, would clearly become goats. Me, I was destined to be a cow.

Today Robyn has three kids, all sunny-faced and red-headed, coppery, the color of her Irish setter, as if the dog had birthed the children and not my Christopher Robin, who is still, despite all the Central Coast sun, sallow and pale like her well-known ancestor, her dark hair like a starless city night. Robyn hosts a blog she calls *My So-Called Life*. I write in sometimes, post in the comments section. I imagine my posts are kind and funny. I like to see how she's doing. She's doing fine, just fine. How could she not? I sign off "Your So-Called Girlfriend."

My father died in 1998, same year as Reagan, same disease. At the end, Dad couldn't even remember that he didn't like me, that he despised the woman I had become. I didn't say anything. Neither did my mother. I thought about it, though, as I sat there at his bedside in my childhood bedroom in the two-bedroom house in Lomita, my chaste twin bed with its *Wizard of Oz* bedspread exiled to the garage, replaced by a rented hospital bed with bars we could raise to keep him safe inside, a giant crib. My parents had otherwise kept the room exactly how I left it. The bottlebrush tree filled the window, its sticky red blossoms framed by curtains imprinted with my favorite runaways, Dorothy and Toto, still making their way to the Emerald City. As I sat there in my desk chair, I considered reminding my dying father of his hurtful words—words that, as a teenager, I had memorized with a kind of angry pride. Those strings of epithets, some true, some not, the words still there between us whenever I saw him. I wondered if he remembered, too, if he still believed what he had said in his seething rages. But at the end he loved me as much as he did when I was a kid, his only kid, his June, his June bug, his beloved bookworm tomboy, years before I grew into some other creature.

Or perhaps he imagined I was one of the cadre of caregivers who had come to feed and change him, those patient and cheerful dark-haired women from the Philippines or Mexico who had also journeyed to this great country of his, just like his wife. After all, they dressed like I did, in simple outfits of utility. And they possessed, at least during working hours, the kind of quiet, capable submission he admired in women. "Oh, I am so glad it's you today," were the last words he said to me, his mouth lifted into a grateful smile. "So glad, so glad."

Tonight I witness something I've never seen before. I look out my loft window and see four guys spray-painting along a wall, each with his own can, moving smoothly, swiftly, but without fear. They're taking their time.

Lately Los Angeles is stained with graffiti from its gutters to its skyscrapers. You know it happens, but you never see it actually happening. You wake up to a fresh wall of fury where none was before. A once-blank soaring overpass now sports an impossible necklace of outrage. A billboard has been disfigured, a delivery truck tagged. The tagging crew below is moving with ease, as if they have been hired to do the job, scrolling out figures that mean something to them and absolutely nothing to me—urban hieroglyphics, deep violets and blues, blacks and greens, the colors of bruises with puddles of red. The letters are obscene and jubilant, fat and bouncy, shaped like sofa cushions or thighs and buttocks, body parts, squatted and bent into an orgy.

It isn't that late. Some of the day's blue still hangs in the west. Robyn and I once did something like this, more than twenty years ago, after Reagan invaded Grenada, but we did our deed in the dead of night, not at dusk. I am certain no one saw. We set out to spray-paint our modest assertion—WAR IS MENSTRUATION ENVY—in dripping red letters across the Westwood Federal Building's parking lot wall. For days after, I was so scared I couldn't go back and look at it even though I longed to see it in broad daylight with people and parked cars, the daily traffic crawl of thousands. By the time I did, our words were gone, painted over with a thick coat of manila-envelope beige, like nothing had ever been there but wall. Someone told me that my friend Teresa Medina had taken a photograph, and that it hung in one of her shows, but I've never seen it. Teresa lives in San Francisco now, and sometimes I think I am the only one left in this city who still remembers what we did and why.

I am still doing my best to live simply. I visit that parking lot of the Federal Building whenever a demonstration is called. I look at that cinderblock wall and imagine our words ghosting through all these years later—WAR IS MENSTRUATION ENVY. I see Robyn standing with her can of fire-alarm red, intent but laughing, full of rage and glee. She is wearing overalls and I am in my usual black leggings and flannel. I remember I was scared, more than usual, but giddy too. The cans seemed to sing—high, tinny—as the paint sprayed. Robyn took the first word and the second and the last, and I took the long single word that makes up the third.

"You're the better speller, June," she told me.

We met at the end of ENVY, kissed, then ran. From what? I wondered, even then. The coast was clear. We held hands as we fled, letting the two cans roll away, my skating boots clacking against the pavement as if it were a lake of asphalt ice.

Now, I imagine that these guys busy below must have had staked out their wall like Robyn and I did, had lookouts and a good sense of how this particular downtown neighborhood goes to sleep early. My neighborhood's changing, gentrifying, like most everything. Gorky's Café is long gone. Wilshire Books is closed, the bearded owner dead, the belly-dancing daughter gone north to grow medical marijuana up in Humboldt. Little Frida's burned down. The stout Black cook who presided over the Irish pub's Indian kitchen, his sweaty face glistening in the doorway, has passed away, a swift heart attack from all that glorious high-cholesterol buttery ghee.

My mother lives simply with me now. My mother! Since my father's death, she seems to have grown younger. She is, of course, just twenty years older than me, same as she always was, but I couldn't see this until my father died. All I saw when I looked at them was my parents and a faraway, almost fairy-tale war, the one he fought in and the one she came from. A distant country responsible for the cherished fringed satin souvenir pillows on the couch and the broad features (cow-like, Robyn's mother might quip) that my mother and I share. But my father was a teenage soldier, and my mother was a child, an orphan, much younger than him, always profoundly grateful for the life she had here—a husband, a child, a house—and silent about where she came from. Now she lives with me, blocks from bustling Koreatown where she seems to have made another life midway through her own, taking the subway to the Buddhist temple and Seoul Peace Park and returning to our shared apartment ten stories above downtown. She shops in the markets and brings home food that is new to me and familiar to her. Dandelion greens, ramps, watercress. She cooks with a kind of attention that is like prayer. If life could indeed be like those feminist tracts that still mean so much to me, my mother is rediscovering herself, and I, her daughter, am finally discovering her. She is the best roommate I have ever had: she pays her bills on time, she says nothing if I stay out all night or return with someone who shares my futon, and she still loves me. Still.

She is out there tonight, making her way home. Below, the guys with the spray paint are still at work, taking on the plywood wall that spans the perimeter fence of the new construction site. Beyond the fence, an enormous hole. COMING SOON, a sign promises, and beneath it, an artist's rendering of a silver geometric building lunges at the sky. I am pleased to see how completely the taggers obliterate the threat.

These guys move like they had nothing to lose, no one to fear. They squat, they bend, they stretch. The street, the wall, the city seems theirs in a way it never was mine even when I marched down its middle, one of thousands shouting: "Whose streets? Our streets." I am still a person who joins the march, puts one foot in front of the other, who believes in the words she chants, who carries signs lettered with impossible demands.

Perhaps these Black and Brown boys working on their wall have lost their own fear or never had much to lose to begin with. Who knows? I am not innocent to what their words may signify. The price of urban affluence and decay. But what was it Jane Jacobs said? Jacobs, who Robyn so admired? I read that big book of hers when I was still trying to follow Robyn where she was going, highlighting passages as if the bright yellow would show me the way. Something about how people must take a degree of public responsibility for each other, even if we have no ties. I am not ignorant of my own innocence back in the day, exaggerating the power of two girls with red paint working in the moonlit shadow of the Federal Building's tower, across the street from the vast silence of the veterans' cemetery where one day my own father would be buried. But still. And yet.

The streetlights pop on, like a chain of cheap bright pearls. That's my mother, making her way down the street. Once Jyeong-soon, then Joanne, finally Mrs. Robert Harper. That's how she signs her name still. Tears in her eyes, she told me that that name is still the most beautiful to her. Still. She is moving with purpose, this slight woman, not yet old, her life not about to be over.

My mother pauses a moment, stops, picks up from the sidewalk what I know must be a coin, a penny, perhaps, and slips it into her skirt pocket with a little pat as if to comfort it. She holds a plastic bag and even from here I can see the green stalks poking out, a bouquet of those spring greens she loves. Her head tilts. She sees the boys at work on the wall. She waits. They're almost done.

Ocean Park #12

Teresa sees that the couch is the same: legless and lime green, hauled up the two flights of stairs by two guys who pulled over when Lola and Teresa still imagined that they could somehow bungee it to the back of Lola's Dodge Dart. Lola enjoyed maintaining they could have done it themselves, but Teresa gave up too soon.

The two young women had spotted the couch in an alley on their way home from a gallery opening where they noshed on cheese cubes and free wine in plastic cups. The show was a bust but the buffet table was worth their time. Melon slices. Strawberries. A Brie that practically wept onto a platter when cut. That is what they liked about their neighborhood and the mid-1980s: the generous street-side haul-away economy that allowed them to furnish their apartment pretty much for free and feed themselves as well. That, and the fact that if you stood on your toes in the shower and glanced out the rectangular window, you could see a slim wedge of the Pacific Ocean; it was only five blocks and one very broad band of sand away. When the car broke down, they could take the Big Blue Bus to the university for 50 cents. It rumbled by the apartment building every hour and dropped them on the campus thirty minutes later.

Nowadays there were city ordinances and restrictions about free booze and free furniture and a new row of candy corn–colored condos across the street that had taken away the ocean view. Teresa hadn't ridden a bus in years, though she heard that Lola had to when things got bad. "Did you know that this was Richard Diebenkorn's old neighborhood? Where he painted his Ocean Park series?" Lola had whispered when they saw the apartment for the first time. Teresa didn't, and she said so. She'd grown up in Torrance, an undistinguished suburb to the south that no one, to her knowledge, had ever painted. Back then, she didn't even know who Diebenkorn was, but she didn't let on.

The two guys had a pickup and time on their hands, and soon Lola and Teresa had a couch and two more mouths to feed that night for dinner. They weren't hungry themselves but fixed spaghetti and opened a cheap bottle of California Merlot and then bade the pair a firm goodnight. They never saw them again, but the legless lime-green couch resides today in the Santa Monica rent-controlled walk-up where Lola still lives. A large framed Diebenkorn reproduction hangs above it, all cool airy oceanic blues and minty greens warmed with purples and yellows, cross-cut with lines. Lola bought it for full price at one of the galleries where they ate for free. Teresa had come to recognize the painting as their neighborhood: the light, the hills, and the houses, even the misty wedge of ocean through the shower window. "Did you know Diebenkorn's studio was near here?" she would say when people came to visit.

It is Teresa's turn to care for Lola and the first time she's been back to the apartment since moving out fifteen years earlier. They hadn't had a falling-out as much as a falling-away, a gradual drift that grew into years and then the ambush of middle age. Teresa's wall map of the Middle East, rescued from the trash bin of a nearby high school, still hangs where she left it, diagonal from the couch and the Diebenkorn. It is a so-called "political map," large and colorful, and takes up most of the wall, equal in size to the window that looks eastward toward the city. Teresa had liked the way the map looked, the brightly colored countries, the blue seas and rivers, the blunt lettering, the borders, how the wooden dowels at the top and bottom gave it a frame. It's art, she'd decided. In the classroom it was something else, but here, on our wall, it's art. Lola agreed.

Then the first Gulf War came and suddenly the map was something else. That January night, when war was officially declared after months of posturing and troop build-ups, Teresa cut out tiny battleships and miniature planes from black construction paper and deployed them with glue in the Persian Gulf and the Indian Ocean. She'd stayed up all night with her X-Acto knife, pressing deeply into the paper until the razor hit the breadboard she was using. When Lola awoke the next morning, the Persian Gulf in their living room was crowded with the American fleet. Later, Teresa added tanks and helicopters, cruise missiles, soldier silhouettes, arrows indicating movements, flags. The war eventually became her MFA thesis project. She photographed the development of the map and the daily combat coverage on television from a tripod set up in the living room in front of the lime-green couch, below the relative peace of the Diebenkorn: a series of glamorous headshots of news anchors with the hostilities flaming behind them and banner headlines crawling below. When the war ended a little more than a month later, her thesis was finished too. For the big MFA show, she scored another castaway couch and placed it in front of the wall where her work hung at the university gallery.

Now, when Teresa returns, flying in from San Francisco, another war is on the television and Lola sits on the green couch, below her Diebenkorn, wrapped in a thrift-store afghan, a stretchy web of bright orange and brown yarn. The deployed artillery and troops remain where Teresa left them on the Middle East map. It is like nothing has changed—except, of course, for Lola's breast cancer and the fact that this particular war has been going on for five years now, and that Teresa doesn't take photos anymore, not of anything.

Twenty years earlier, Teresa stole Lola's shampoo and conditioner. Lola's products had always seemed better than her own. The bottles and tubes in the shower were full of chemicals that Teresa disavowed publicly but, standing in the private steam, she read the lists of ingredients and the directions with an eagerness that she found more embarrassing than the theft. *Silk amino acids. Calcium gluconate. Dimethicone.* Her own earnest organic hair products cost nearly the same but lacked French subtitles and mysterious chemical formulas. She squirted the fluids into her palm and followed the directions on the bottles with care, as if by doing so she might achieve the same beautiful black tresses as her roommate—long, thick, and lustrous, like a fairy-tale princess. *Shampoo, rinse, condition, wait, rinse, repeat.* While the fortifying emollients worked their magic, replenishing her stressed hair, restoring her moisture balance, amplifying her limp roots, Teresa stood on her toes in the shower and peeped out the narrow window to study their ocean view. There was something soothing in this hopeful ritual, though the results, if any, were imperceptible. Teresa told herself it was because she didn't use Lola's products as regularly as the bottles advised. They left a tangy citrus scent. Unmistakable. Teresa used to worry. Would Lola know? Could she tell? Whenever Lola was in the apartment when she showered, Teresa used her own shampoo, emerging from the bathroom with her dark hair smelling like pine cones.

Now her former roommate has no hair, no eyelashes, no eyebrows, just a feeble blond fuzz under the black wig. "I don't know why it's coming in like that," Lola said on the phone, "but it's sort of cool to finally be a blond." Showering late this afternoon, Teresa sees those same bottles, the expensive hair care products that she still never buys for herself. Top of the line, standing on the windowsill, making their promises. When she reaches for them, she sees the dust that has collected in the crevices of the plastic caps and on the shoulders of the smooth bottles, notes the congealed drips, and Teresa hasn't the heart to squeeze, to pour, to massage her roots even though Lola has called a bouncy encouragement through the door: "Use anything you want!"

Did Lola always know? Teresa wonders. Did she always know and say nothing? But for once, Teresa doesn't steal, doesn't take what isn't hers, just stands in the strong spray and lets the water wash her. A bit overwhelmed, she begins to weep. She pushes up on her toes to look out the window but instead of the ocean, she sees the new condos across the street and a man poised at a smoky barbeque on his patio. He talks to someone on the cell phone he holds in one hand and pokes some kind of grilled meat using a long fork with the other. It's almost dinner time. Her hair, when she towels it, is rough. It's going to look like hell.

Teresa wraps herself in a thick white towel. Even Lola's linens were always better than hers, those big loops, the weight and size, the white brilliance. Although Teresa has stopped crying, she knows her eyes are red. But she can't hide them; she has nowhere else to go except to Lola. She doesn't live here anymore, after all. There's no bedroom to retreat to, no job to be late for and run out the door. Besides, the whole reason she's here is to take care of Lola. When Teresa opens the bathroom door and steps into the coolness of the hallway, Lola is there, on her right, in the bedroom that used to be Teresa's and is now Lola's home studio. It's a bright room, gets the morning sun best through two curtainless windows. Now, late in the day, Lola has turned on the lights.

She is at her easel, propped on a stool, working on the latest in a series she calls "Inventory." She pauses what she's doing, which is daubing a layer of a soft acrylic green to the background. This one is a close-up of her hairbrush, the strands of her once long black hair nested in its bristles, its curvy handle as pink as bubblegum. Another large painting leans against the far wall. It must be five feet by eight, nearly as big as the futon Teresa once put there. In its center Lola has painted an enormous glass jar, cylindrical and open at the top, filled with pristine white tampons, each individually wrapped in clear cellophane and belted with an aqua tear strip. From afar, the effect is of an old-fashioned candy jar, brimming with promise. Think Wayne Thiebaud in a pharmacy. A Venice gallery is slated to show the series once Lola has depicted each and every item from her medicine cabinet. Sketches are taped to the walls: toothpaste and toothbrush; a collection of plastic prescription bottles clustered like votive candles, tinged with ochre crayon; an eyebrow pencil, its tiny sharpener surrounded by curly wood shavings with red borders. Lola had confided that she knew her cancer was the reason she'd finally scored the solo show after all these years. "But I'll take it," she said with a short laugh. "Why not? I'll give them some blood on the toothbrush. That kind of thing. That's what they want."

Now Lola asks, "What's up?" She's wearing black leggings, a big T-shirt, oversized socks, a red bandana tied pirate-style on her fuzzy head. Her wig, a shinier synthetic version of her hair as it used to be, hangs on top of a floor lamp, an unlikely lampshade. She sees Teresa looking at it. "Don't worry. I don't turn on the light," Lola says. "I just really can't stand wearing it while I work. Then my head gets cold and, well, the scarf is best." She looks at Teresa again. "But what's wrong? Something's wrong."

This is not what Teresa came here to do but she hears herself start talking and she doesn't know how to stop. "I'm sorry," she says, cold now and growing colder wearing only Lola's fancy towel. "I have to tell you . . . I used to steal your shampoo and conditioner." Her voice actually cracks and she begins to tear up again.

Lola starts to laugh. She doesn't put the brush down but holds it high, and the smile she cracks seems to split her face in two. "Oh, no. Not you too! Man, you wouldn't believe how many people call up and apologize or confess since the diagnosis. Crying just like you. But don't worry. Besides," Lola goes on, "I knew you were all along. I thought you did it because I was putting the moves on Mark. I was so incorrigible, wasn't I? Anyway, I thought it was some kind of reimbursement you were extracting—revenge, refund, payback. Right, right?" She doesn't wait for an answer but returns to the canvas and smears the green forcefully.

The paint is the color of toothpaste, of fluoride, Teresa thinks, not that she knows if fluoride has a color, but if it did it would be this pharmaceutical green.

"Don't worry," Lola continues, "all is forgiven. Really, I can afford to be generous. All you took was shampoo. Me, I took your boyfriend. Or at least a piece of him." She smiles, then grimaces. "That was bad. I'm sorry. I was bad, I know. So bad. I should be the one to apologize. You know that Mark has been so good since I got sick. So good. I always knew he cared." Her brushstrokes become short, steady, drumming.

This doesn't seem right to Teresa. She was always exquisitely, painfully aware of Mark's trespasses. And there were many, but she is quite certain Lola wasn't among them. She adjusts the towel edge, tucking it deeper into her armpit. Lord knows she knew who Lola slept with. The walls in the apartment were thin. Besides, Teresa thought they were close, too close for secrets this big.

"I should have apologized to you long ago," Lola says. "But I knew you understood. I was drinking so much those days, so out of control. I did a lot of shit I shouldn't. I should have made it right when I was doing my steps. I'm sorry." Lola does look sorry. Her lashless blue eyes have suddenly acquired pink rims. She has put down the paintbrush and crossed her legs, balancing on the stool. "It's good you're here," she says. "Means a lot."

Teresa is confused. She doesn't remember Lola drinking any more than anyone else. They all drank, but if she were to make a list of the people she knew likely to have drinking problems, Lola wouldn't be on it. "You're in AA?" Teresa asks.

Lola nods. "Two years," she says. "Weekly meetings down at the church. My sponsor is some Vietnam War vet, a retired special ed teacher from the high school." She rolls her eyes. "Old but kinda cute. Drives a jeep. That's my world. Can you imagine?"

No, Teresa thinks, I can't imagine. "You're sober?" she asks.

Lola nods again. "Hard to imagine, huh?" Her smile returns, all cheerful pride.

"I mean, of course you are *now*," Teresa says. "You *have* to be. But I didn't know you had a drinking problem. I mean, if you had a drinking problem, then I did. We all did. I never thought you were a drunk. Come on." She is trying not to think about Mark, what that might mean and why she should care.

Lola just looks at her. "Thanks," she says finally, the smile swallowed, her voice carefully even. "But I know who I was and what I did. I believe some of my behavior, some of *our* behavior, contributed to where I am now. My situation."

"I'm sorry," Teresa says, backing off as quickly as she can. "I shouldn't have said that. I was surprised, that's all. Good for you. Sobriety. Yes. I should get dressed." She tugs at the towel and hopes she looks sheepish. "We should eat. I'll get dinner going. I'm sorry."

"It's okay," Lola says. And it is as if something that dimmed for a moment has switched back on inside her. She is as bright as ever. She picks up the brush and swivels toward the canvas.

⁂

The next morning the black wig is back on, but Lola still appears vaguely pirate-y in black leggings, oversized white shirt, Doc Martens laced with red tartan laces. It must be something in her attitude, a persistent jauntiness. "I'll be all right," she insists. "To tell you the truth, I prefer doing this part alone. I'll need you more later. Really." She's getting herself and her large bag out of Teresa's rental car. She's got a sketch pad and pencils, CD player and music, extra clothing. Her bag is as big as the carry-on Teresa packed for the weekend.

Teresa has pulled over in the roundabout of the university medical center. "You sure?"

"Yes." The answer is firm but comes with a smile. "I'll call you when the infusion's done. You should hang out here. Visit our old stomping grounds, that sort of thing. You get a discount at the coffeehouse if you say you're a student. I do. They don't ask for ID. They've got an espresso machine now."

Someone honks and Lola slams the car door. She waves and then she's gone through the hospital doors.

⁂

Teresa pays full price for her caffè latte. When the lanky barista asks if she's a student, she answers, "I used to be, is that good enough?"

Apparently not. Before she finishes, the young man has already hit a button and so she hands over a $5 bill and pushes the change he gives her in the tip jar. He still doesn't crack a smile. "I studied photography," she offers. "How about you?" She pegged him for psychology. Something about the button-up shirt, the quick judgment.

"You still take pictures?" he asks.

"No," she says.

"What a waste," he says, handing over a tall, steaming paper cup. "Lids are over there." He points to a counter and slides his eyes to the next customer in line.

It's Friday near the end of spring quarter. The campus is nearly empty. Teresa heads off to where she knew she'd be going all along, making her way past the familiar buildings of red- and cream-colored brick. She used to wait for Mark in the university sculpture garden, a sudden pocket of space and light between the buildings—watch him striding across the green beneath the purple blooms of the jacaranda trees, pausing to slap the ass of the monumental nude standing woman if he felt particularly good. Lola never liked the garden, too obviously pretty. Teresa loved it, though perhaps what she liked best was waiting there for Mark.

She settles on a shaded bench in the corner. The garden is almost the same except the trees are larger. Today the purple blossoms have fallen on the grass, surrounding the tree trunks like full skirts. A child is exploring a twiggy bronze horse that Teresa hasn't seen before. Must be new. Two parents are at a distance, sitting on a bench, focused on their cell phones.

She pulls out her own. She knows the name of Mark's firm and, after a brief conference with the operator, she makes a connection. Reception is startlingly clear. The secretary asks her name and the nature of her business.

"Teresa Medina," she says "You can tell him it's old business." She likes that, the *Robert's Rules of Order* sound of it, how it conjures meetings and satisfies the secretary's professional curiosity. When Mark picks up, she's still laughing.

Mark had married a few years back, a much younger woman who nobody knew. Charmaine. A blond, Teresa noted, still taking notes. Lola and Teresa called her Chardonnay. Everybody in the old gang was invited to the wedding, but Teresa hadn't been up for it. Too soon. Eventually Mark and Chardonnay had twin girls but gave them names that Teresa took for boys' names. She'd imagined them as miniature Marks in overalls with yellow Tonka trucks. Even now it's hard for her to think of Madison and Hayden as girls—more likely a powdered wig president and the longhaired founder of SDS. Last year Lola had seen Chardonnay quoted in a newspaper article, "Beyond the Bounce House," about the challenges of keeping up with upscale birthday parties. "It gets harder every year," she had complained, and then went on to describe her latest celebration, which involved renting a stable of ponies and a trick cowboy rider. Lola had clipped it out and mailed it to Teresa, "No comment" scrawled across the top. The last time Teresa had seen Mark was just before his wedding, before she got the design job with health benefits and good money, two weeks paid vacation, those things that seemed important then, and moved north to the Bay Area, the place she told everyone she had always wanted to live. Mark had been behind her at a stoplight somewhere on the Westside. She was startled when she recognized him in the rearview mirror in a sports utility vehicle, a Tonka for adults. Mark's mouth hung open. He didn't see her. He was always a mouth breather, she thought.

"Teresa. Hey, babe, how's it going?" Mark had the annoying habit of using endearments with ex-girlfriends whether they wanted them or not. "You got in last night?"

"I just dropped her off," Teresa says. "She didn't want me to come in for the chemo."

"Same with me," he replies. "How does she seem to you?"

"Well, bald, sort of blond, skinny."

"Yeah, well, what else? Why'd you call? Money? I already sent my share for this month. Everybody else is paid up. Does she need more?"

Lola had taken her stage 4 diagnosis with characteristic aplomb. "Everybody gets something. This is what I get," she quipped in that first phone call. Her friends rallied to create a support network. She didn't have a family like most of them did, no parents or siblings ready to swoop in. Her freelance career lacked health insurance, but connections helped. Everyone wrote checks. A musician friend turned social worker got her set up in a special program at the university medical center. June supervised meal deliveries. Volunteers slept over on chemo weekends. Mark coordinated it all, though Teresa assumed it was really his secretary who set up the calendar and sent out reminders. He was never that organized. Still, Mark made it happen. He did, as Lola suggested, really care.

"No, it's not money." She tells him and waits in the ensuing silence. The latte is finally cool enough to gulp. She gulps.

"You can tell me," she says. "I won't get mad. Not now. Not anymore. I don't even know why I care but I do. So," she sighs, "did you ever mess around with Lola?" Feeling foolish, she describes the previous day's encounter, Lola's chatty animated confession. The child is now beating the bronze horse with a stick.

Mark gives her his adamant lawyer tone: "Never happened," he declares. "I'm as confused as you."

"Really?" she asks but she doesn't have to. She believes him. Mark always confessed infidelities right away. It was so annoying.

"Really."

"Okay. Now, one more thing. Did Lola ever have a drinking problem?" Once again she feels foolish, asking questions she knows the answers to.

"Lo? Come on."

"Yeah, that's what I thought. But she says she did. That she's in AA too. Done all the steps. Going around asking forgiveness from people. Sober for years, she says."

"Maybe it's the drugs," Mark says, "the chemo. I read about a side effect, chemo brain. Maybe that's where this is coming from."

"Maybe." Teresa is slow to agree and now she's quiet.

"Let it go, babe. Don't say anything."

"You're still telling me what to do?" Her voice has a charge to it, but she knows he's right.

They talk a bit more. She asks after the twins (*Girls! girls!* she reminds herself, *girls with boys' names*) who are older than she had calculated them being. "Must be great," she says, meaning it despite herself. Why not? she thinks, let his life be great, this part of it, anyway. He lives north of Montana now, where the bougie people live. He's got what he wants.

She remembers the night during the first war when the two of them stole into the sculpture garden and shrouded all the figures in black cotton sacks. Mark's favorite monumental nude transformed into a massive mourner. She took photographs as the sun came up. Mark watched her work from where she now sits, holding vending machine coffees for them both, one in each hand. She took a photo of him too, unshrouded, the steaming cups held like sacraments, but it didn't come out.

"It is," he replies. "Just great."

"I'm sorry about the bunny," she says, surprising herself. But the time seems right for another overdue apology. One thing AA got right was the need to atone. At least she's apologizing for things she actually did. First the shampoo, now the rabbit.

"The what?"

"The big bunny. Your," she pauses, "wedding present." She feels herself blush, though no one is near enough to notice.

Teresa had purchased the outsized plaster of paris lawn ornament as a wedding gift. The white bunny stood nearly six feet tall (taller than Mark, Lola had pointed out) and had a maniacal look in its purple eyes. It wore blue overalls and carried a pitchfork. She bought it at an outlet store on Fairfax where it had been marked down five different times, and by the time she saw it, the giant hare had been pushed so far to the front of the store it was almost in the street. "I'll take it," she told the girl behind the counter. "Can I have it delivered?" The delivery charge cost more than the rabbit.

"Oh, that," Mark says with a little laugh that sounds like a cough. "You mean Harvey?"

They both laughed.

"Yes, the pooka. I don't know what got into me," she says, not quite the truth but close enough.

"That's okay. We ended up putting it in the backyard. The girls love it, especially at Easter. They get their pictures taken with it and everything. Don't apologize. It worked out."

Lola had been right. She needed Teresa later. She was fine in the car, triumphant, bragging about how today, after weeks of chemo hell, she was finally, finally able to nail a good sketch of her chemo bag, complete with the word *peligro*. But somewhere on the 10, heading west, whatever was keeping her going vanished. Once they pulled into the carport, she opened the car door, moved her legs out, placed both feet firmly on the ground and then just sat there, leaning over as if she were tying the plaid laces of her Docs. Teresa heard something pour out and create a puddle on the ground.

"Where are those two dudes in the pickup?" Lola asked. She sounded like she was smiling but Teresa couldn't see her face. The wig had fallen like a curtain. The words came out with effort, each one needing a breath.

"We can do it ourselves," Teresa told her.

She ended up carrying Lola, first up the flight of stairs from the carport, then the two flights of stairs to the apartment. Lola didn't want anything, just a bath, she said, so Teresa ran one and sat on the floor beside the tub, on the little blue mat, adding warm water when it grew cool, sprinkling in aromatherapy salts as needed. She tried not to look at the incision across the left breast, the port implanted beneath her shoulder, jutting through her skin, the pale, whittled, hairless body. Lola's wearily downcast "I'm sorry" seemed to cover everything, and whatever Teresa might have said or not said didn't matter. So she did as Mark advised: she let it go. Lola was sorry. Sorry, apparently, for everything, if Teresa wanted to take it that way. Mark had prepared her for the worst but when that happened, in between the hour-long bath and bed, it wasn't as bad as seeing Lola just sink deep inside herself and go somewhere else.

❧

That night Teresa wakes up. She's on the lime-green couch, and even though the sheets are six hundred thread count (she couldn't help herself; she looked at the label,) and she's tired, she can't fall back to sleep. She turns on the TV but finds reruns of last night's news. The war correspondents are touted as "live from the field," but this is false. She saw the footage hours ago. Not that much has changed. Besides, how much difference can a few hours make? The two local men killed in separate incidents involving roadside bombs at 11 P.M. are still just as dead at 2 A.M. Their two young widows are still both named Nicole and the babies born to each soldier will still grow up without their fathers.

She gets up and steps down the hall to check on Lola, who must have awakened too, then fallen asleep again. The television in her bedroom is on, the sound turned low. "A gift from Mark," Lola had said. "He came over and installed it himself." Teresa doesn't believe her, can't imagine Mark with a drill and a screwdriver, but there it is. The TV hangs high in the corner for easy viewing from the bed. The war is in here too. Lola sleeps, wrapped in white sheets and a white comforter, propped on pillows, wearing a big white T-shirt. The televised war with its patriotic palette illuminates her, flickers on her pale skin, on the tumbled, wide white bed. The red, the blue, the blast of orange light up Lola's bed as if it's on fire. It's an image Teresa wishes she could photograph: the body in bed with its own quiet brutal internal fire, the torn bodies on television, the hushed blue background glow. Once she would have been in here clicking away with her Minolta, but now she just stands and watches.

Was Lola an alcoholic? Had she slept with Mark? Wanted to? Was she just saying it now to somehow make it true? Make the past better in light of the admissions? Different? Is that what people did? And why does it matter so much to her? It seemed some people said things whether or not they did them or believed them. They just said them. Maybe repeated them until they believed. Then apologized for what never happened or defended what didn't exist. While what had really happened went unatoned for.

Lola's cancer. There it is. And the war, well, there it is as well. No matter what it came from, you couldn't argue it didn't exist now. But why? And what to do? Teresa knows that she hasn't done enough. She never could. She'll have to do more. In two days she'll be back home, and Lola will be here alone, sleeping alone in her big white bed, the war still shining its lights and lies on her, her body fighting itself. Teresa knows what it is like to sleep alone; she is reconciled to it, but it must be different when you're where Lola is. She wonders when Lola last slept with someone, if she knew then it was the last time, if it actually will be.

When Teresa climbs into the bed, Lola doesn't wake but her body seems to know someone is close. She curls into Teresa, and Teresa, with some awkwardness, puts her arm around her until her hand reaches Lola's back, the thin shirt, the bones she knows she's going to feel. She's finally in that bed, Lola's bed, whose noises she used to listen to, she must admit, with some kind of jealousy and desire. Lola still smells faintly of the bath, of her pricey lemon and mint salts.

She should have turned the television off. She can't reach the remote from where she is and knows she won't fall asleep like this. The television blazes. A reporter in a flak jacket once again explains how the suicide bomber triggered the exploding vest that killed sixty-five people in an open market. Soon it will be the two dead local men, their widows, their fatherless children. If she wants to sleep, Teresa will have to get up. How could anybody fall asleep watching the war, she wonders, unless, of course, like Lola, they were dying too?

Some Final Beauty

"I thought the shop always sent two," remarked the mortuary staffer as he helped Toni tug out the twin floral wreaths and the two easels. "And a van."

Toni had done her best with her decade-old Subaru, folding the backseat and sliding the empty passenger seat as far forward as it could go, anything to accommodate the heart-shaped wreaths and their stands. Even so, the lilies on one of the wreaths were crushed. Water had sloshed out of the tapered black plastic bucket wedged behind the driver's seat that held dozens of long-stemmed white roses. In the summer heat, her car smelled like old vase water.

She recognized the young man from the service at the meetinghouse. With his sun-blasted blond hair and deep tan, he looked as if he would have been happier jockeying for a wave in the lineup at Swami's than in his serviceable black chinos and button-down shirt. He stood in the back while his veteran colleague, a tall officious woman who had mastered the tone of respectful mourning, made all the official announcements at the official moments: *Will the family please join us in the viewing room for final goodbyes? The family invites you to join them for a repast on the patio before proceeding to the cemetery. The hearse will be leaving before your departure. Please follow the printed directions to Tierra Linda cemetery*. Apparently, her assistant hadn't pegged stoic Toni as a family member of the funeral party, a relation of her more obviously distraught sister, Dolores, the sorrowful grandmother. Why would he? Everyone wore black. Most were masked. In her simple black dress, she could have been anybody. She liked that. There was comfort in that, escape.

"You know," she replied with a weary exaggerated sigh, "the pandemic. No one wants to work." The words were so easy to say. And just like that, Toni was a florist.

"Tell me about it," he said. "We should have had two more guys with us for the offloading." He jerked his head toward the white casket, suspended above the prepared gravesite, the darkness below hidden by a bright green Astroturf blanket. "We got the groundskeepers to help. Nice guys." The groundskeepers in question had retreated to the distant far side of the cemetery, where they waited. This was to be the final committal of the summer day.

Tierra Linda was a small cemetery in a part of the county that Toni had never visited despite, like her grieving sister, spending the entirety of her life there. As directed, she took the freeway, the one named for the famous all-American baseball player with the unacknowledged Mexican mother, as in from Mexico, which turned into a two-lane parkway and finally this, a well-graded dirt road lined with stables and a small rodeo arena and, at its dead end, the wrought iron gates of the cemetery. It was at the edge of one of those sprawling green and lush San Diego towns that disappeared into dust just before it hit the dry hills. The grounds looked as if they'd been a horse property at one time, with mature oaks and sycamores offering some dappled shade, quaint white fencing. One sweep of her gaze could see it all, not like those epic burial parks amid rolling green hills that bordered the freeways back in the city. The headstones here were old and new, large and small, white and gray, the color of old silver. Her older sister Dolores wasn't wrong when she had said it was pretty.

It was all of twenty minutes from the suburban strip mall where the Mormon meetinghouse stood, a repurposed former savings and loan facility that now served the needs of the ward in the eastern part of the county. The onetime bank's architecture seemed well suited to its new identity as a community church. The chapel's peculiar airy sense of transaction was heightened once Toni realized that the rostrum from which the services were conducted was the place where the tellers had once stood, doling out and receiving monies. She surmised that the private viewing room where the family had gathered before the coffin was closed had once served a similar function for clients with safe-deposit boxes. It all made sense.

Before this morning, Toni had never visited a Mormon meetinghouse, though the faith's embrace by her sister's daughter Brenda and then Brenda's daughter Sophie acquainted her with some of the faith's traditions. Planetary afterlife. Special underwear. No caffeine. No alcohol. Food storage for the coming end times. The preferred use of the term Saints rather than Mormons. And, like the Catholics, no ordination for women; instead, lots of babies. Temples, as she and her sister learned, could be entered only by those baptized and in good standing in the faith. So Sophie's Celebration of Life could not be held in one of those grand white architectural confections topped by a gilded Angel Moroni and his trumpet, not just because of the young woman's fallen status, but because of her family, long lapsed Catholics.

Toni had been mildly hopeful that "the girls," as she always called Brenda and Sophie, might find some kind of much-needed stability with the Latter-Day Saints. At least that's what she told people. They needed stability, those two. Brenda, who'd become a single mother at fifteen, acted more like her daughter's pal than a parent. Sophie was quick to grow up and become her young mother's shadow. Truth be told, Toni wondered if the Mormons would survive the two girls. They were wild. Wilder than anything Dolores and Toni had ever imagined, had ever been themselves. It was likely, though, that the LDS church would be just fine. Her niece Brenda and Brenda's daughter Sophie not so much.

"Where do you want these?" Surfer Boy asked. He held the two easels, still folded, in his arms.

Toni cradled a crumpled wreath while trying to coax the crushed calla lilies back into shape. She summoned a businesslike tone. "One at either end, of course," she said curtly, a little unkindly, as if he should know better, as if she did. "One at the foot, one at the head." Sophie's feet, Sophie's head; such tiny feet, such long hair, she began to think, then she stopped. The thick curving petals of the lilies felt like old skin against her fingers, and yet Sophie was only twenty-four years old.

"Sorry," he said. "I'm still new."

"I can tell," she sniffed.

Toni found it impossible to tell anyone at work that her sister's granddaughter was the one who had died. Whose granddaughter just dies? She applied for the three-day bereavement leave the company offered all employees and was relieved that the HR platform that tracked and tallied everyone didn't demand details. The pandemic's work-from-home edict also reduced inquiries. Toni would be surprised if anyone actually noticed she was gone.

Had she been at the office, Toni would have made up some

story, partly true, partly false. No one really wants to hear that any twenty-four-year-old anywhere has died of a fentanyl overdose and all the sad details that invariably accompany such a tale. Better COVID, which, technically, Sophie had—*of course she did*—but it was the drugs that were, what did they call it? the precipitating cause? Trigger? COVID-19 just sealed the deal.

The COVID diagnosis was convenient, actually, her niece Brenda had confided to Toni breathlessly at the hospital vending machines days earlier. *Did Aunt Toni know that with COVID on the death certificate FEMA would pay for the funeral, up to $9,000? What a jackpot! This would cover the service, the casket, plot, headstone, even flowers! Isn't that great?*

No, Aunt Toni hadn't known that. She looked at her niece, or what was left of her niece. Brenda was talking in a cheerful, rapid-fire speedy way, all the while scanning the vending machine for something that probably wasn't even for sale. This woman who had lost her child. Is there a name for a mother who has lost a child, some equivalent of widow or orphan? Toni had given her some cash, some small bills, but now she understood that Brenda would not spend it on food, that she would just pretend to. This was a lesson she had to learn over and over. What Brenda really wanted couldn't be bought at the vending machines or the hospital cafeteria. No one knew where Brenda lived these days, not even her ex-husband, Gideon Layton, the onetime Mormon missionary who had shown up at the door of her Section 8 apartment and fallen for her, Brenda, teenage single mother of little Sophie, as he tried to save her. And for a while he had. They married, sealed for all time in a service in Utah at the Cedar City temple that neither Toni nor her sister Dolores were allowed to attend. They had a child, a boy, Jaco. Sophie had a loving stepfather, a younger half brother. Gideon and Brenda made a life that, for a time, looked like everyone else's.

It was difficult to reconcile the stout but petite babbling woman in front of her, dressed in torn black leggings and a long-sleeved hoodie with the baby she'd held over the baptismal font years ago, the girl she'd watched tumble fearlessly on gym mats, flip between balance bars, and stick her landing. Something had happened. What? A bad crowd. Drugs. Boys. More drugs. Perhaps the inheritance of addiction that no faith could heal. These days her ex Gideon thought Brenda was living in her car again. Dolores had seen her twice at the Mira Mesa farmers' market, panhandling. Brenda had become someone you drove by, walked by, and tried not to see. There were so many of them, but you weren't supposed to recognize them, weren't supposed to be related.

Soon Brenda would be showing up at Tierra Linda with the entourage that had accompanied her to the service. They were equal in number to Gideon's oddly buoyant family, which had flown in from Cedar City, Utah, his troop of toothy brothers and sisters and his aging stately parents. Gideon was the baby. Toni hoped that the Layton clan would take Gideon and Jaco back with them. Jaco had grown up since she'd seen him last and stood taller than his tall father, a handsome, tidy boy who lived on the spectrum. At the service, Jaco had sung with his handsome father and uncles, his voice a sweet unwavering tenor, but before and after the hymn, he interrupted the program by repeatedly barking questions: *Why did my sister die? Why are people crying? Why are you sad? When will this be over?* The answers given did not console the boy, who rocked in the pew between his Utah grandparents, pulling at the brown suit that set uncomfortably on his big body as if to rend it. Jaco had been there with Gideon when Sophie's boyfriend had brought her home, already unconscious, and left her on the couch, saying something about her drinking too much and needing sleep. By the time the EMTs arrived with their Naloxone, it was too late. Jaco had seen it all. Sophie lived for five days on a ventilator in the COVID ward.

Successful at last in reviving the crushed lilies, Toni slipped in some fresh roses and baby's breath where it was needed. She was getting good at this. There was nothing to it. The casket was now framed by the twin hearts and covered with a modest spray of pink and white roses. You might think she'd been doing this her whole life. She turned her attention to the long-stemmed roses remaining in the tall bucket. White buds kissed with pink, some tight, others beginning to unfurl. Dolores had said something about putting one on each chair. It took no time to distribute them on the dozen chairs crowded under the pop-up tent. Plenty were left over, four, five, maybe six dozen. Someone had miscounted. How? Who had imagined there would be more mourners? Three dozen, max, at the meetinghouse, maybe two dozen would come to the graveside. She dragged the bucket away and to the side, close to a cement bench, and sat. It was high-summer hot, but the stone was cool, out of the sun. Surfer Boy had retreated to the shade of a nearby sycamore and was scrolling through his phone.

His colleague approached her, appraising the setup. "Looks good," the woman said. Unlike her coworker, she sported a sleek magnetic nametag on her jacket: *Julie Crawford, Funeral Director.* "Taking those back to the shop?" She pointed at the leftover roses.

Toni began to imagine the flower shop that did not exist, the florist that she did not work for—but then again, in this moment, she did. A soothing fantasy. The refrigerated cases where the leftover roses would be returned. She could use them for another funeral or even a wedding. Roses like this, properly cared for, lasted for days. She could walk through Old Town or Balboa Park and sell them stem by stem to tourists for 5 bucks a pop. She shook her head. "I have orders to use them all, hand them out to people as they arrive and then send the remainder home with the family." She smiled blankly. It felt good to be unmasked in the open air.

"Well, I don't think *this* crowd would even notice what you did." Julie gave a little snort. "Besides, you know they didn't pay for any of this, right?"

"Someone did," Toni offered.

"Yeah, taxpayers did, you and me. What a scam." Another snort. She glanced at the phone in her hand. "They're late. No surprises there. Mind if I smoke?"

Toni shook her head. She was surprised that people still smoked cigarettes, yet they did.

The cigarette encouraged Julie to talk. *Had Toni ever seen such a thing? The sober Mormons and the junkie freaks? What a circus. That big kid screeching? That mother reaching in the coffin to take off her daughter's jewelry and pocket it? That inappropriate eulogy by the stepdad? The dead girl was a stripper, and he talked about how much she liked fashion? And that clueless "Child of God" song? "Rich blessings are in store so I can live with him once more"?*

Toni had seen it all, of course. She was grateful that strangers like Julie hadn't noticed even more. But funeral director Julie hadn't seen Toni, hadn't placed her in one group or another, the Saints or the sinners, because, of course, she belonged to neither. She belonged with her sister Dolores, neither LDS nor addict, just a grandmother who had lost her granddaughter and sat with the remains of her own family. Her ex-husband Ray, the estranged grandfather, drove in from Barstow out of obligation, purchasing a tree online to be planted somewhere in honor of a girl he hadn't seen since she was ten. Ray brought along his latest wife, who leaned into him and squeezed his leg throughout the service. They all sat together in a pew surrounded by a few old friends who had known them back then and had somehow stayed in touch and still cared enough to show up, if not for the lost girl, then for her bereaved, confused grandparents. The two girls they had known and loved, Brenda and her Sophie, had been gone for a long time.

Julie had moved on to a withering critique of the boxed lunch repast and the absence of caffeine and alcohol. "The perks of my job are few," she complained, "and the days are long. At least give me some iced tea or a Coke. A beer, if I'm lucky, or a glass of wine, sometimes champagne."

A whistle from Surfer Boy alerted them to the arrival of the first vehicles.

Julie leaned down and doused her burning cigarette in a flower bucket. She left it floating there and stood up, straightening her jacket. "Jason," she called out, then a sing-songy reprimand: "I don't see the Kleenex boxes." She held up two fingers and jerked her thumb toward the hearse. "Showtime, flower girl," she said with a wink. "Here comes the bride."

As it happened, Toni had been the flower girl at her sister Dolores's wedding to Ray. That wedding photo now seemed to capture the final intact moment of their little family. All of their hope, the last of their hope. The flowers were white roses then too. Little Toni, doing what she'd been told by her own mother, saved one wedding rose for years, wrapped in pink tissue paper, a quiet wrinkled rustle tucked away in her underwear drawer. One day it was gone. She suspected her mother had tossed it, the dried rose that lasted longer than the marriage. On their rare visits, the Laytons always seemed to look around for the rest of their family, but there was none. Father long gone, mother dead. Just Dolores and Toni and Dolores's girls. Toni was never going to add to the world. She saw what it had done. Dolores was different. Toni thought of that lost memento as she handed out the roses one at a time to the mourners approaching the gravesite. She had donned her mask again, but the careful little speech she recited came through clearly: "The family would like you to have a rose to remember Sophie by, or to leave at her grave if you wish."

People seemed pleased. The flowers gave their hands something to do. It gave them a decision to make. They smiled, thanked her. Toni doubted any recognized her. Why would they? The years gone by plus the pandemic mask made a perfect camouflage for the nondescript middle-aged woman she had become. For her part, she didn't know who anyone was either.

Jaco, who didn't meet her eyes, who never had, who perhaps never would, took two, clenching one in each sweaty hand, and marched to the casket, circling it as if he were an honor guard soldier on solemn duty. Outside, in the park-like open air of the cemetery, he was calmer. His incessant questions ceased. She watched as he discarded his jacket, vest, and dress shirt. In his undershirt and trousers he looked like the boy he once had been, soft and shy. Gideon's height and build, Brenda's dark features.

Toni moved around the group, which was bigger than she anticipated, but that was the Mormons for you: they turned out, were polite, grateful for long-stemmed roses. Meanwhile, Brenda and her friends were just driving through the big gates.

Dolores, who had arrived with some of the Layton clan, was also grateful, relieved to see her sister. She walked fitfully, as if she didn't trust the ground beneath her feet. Her eyes above her mask were teary, tired. Toni guided her to a white plastic chair under the canopy's bare square of shade. "Sit," she directed.

"Thanks for taking care of everything," Dolores whispered. In order to pay for everything—casket, plot, headstone, transportation, death certificates, and the services—Dolores bought the flowers on the cheap. Delivery only. No setup. That FEMA money actually went only so far. She had asked Toni to make it work.

"I better get back to it," Toni said. "You sit here." She didn't want to leave her sister, but she didn't want to stay either. The pop-up tent was filling up with the aged and devout, and Toni, the heathen, began to fear the inevitable overtures from the saved. She still couldn't tell if anyone actually knew who she was; however, she recalled that soul crusaders were not picky. The unsaved were fair game. That's how Gideon had snagged Brenda, then Sophie. Best to return to her flower bucket, her new career.

Brenda was heading her way, racing up the green hill in great strides. Toni grasped why she was late as soon as she came closer. She wore the same torn black leggings and the same tight long-sleeved hoodie she'd worn to the service, but obviously she'd had a little something and was fully flying now, her round face gleaming with a stoned manic glee. A dozen members of Brenda's congregation, Sophie's friends and hers, trailed behind, singly and in pairs. Some of the amped-up ones lingered at headstones, draping themselves over the monuments, posing, taking photos with their phones. Two men crouched behind one, looking intently at something no one else could see. One began to wander with purpose among the graves, collecting the small American flags that still remained from the Fourth of July. Compared to the modest dress of Gideon and his family, Brenda's friends were indeed a circus, as Julie Crawford claimed. A swarming, roiling carnival of brightly streaked hair and strategically exposed skin, tattooed limbs and costume-y clothing, both gothic and clownish, verging on the obscene.

It was hard to look away, but to look too closely was to observe, notice, apprehend too much: the discolored teeth, the cheap wraparound sunglasses, the deeply filthy feet stuffed in fuzzy bedroom slippers or flip-flops, the universal long sleeves of everyone in the pack, worn to cover needle tracks, the sweaty pungent restlessness of all. If the LDS contingent were calmly certain in the face of death because of their respectful distance from it, demarcated in marble and reassuring scripture, their counterparts flirted recklessly with it because it was so close and so available. Brenda ran past Toni on the way to Jaco who, having seen her, began to jump up and down and wail. The rest grabbed roses from the bucket before Toni could even offer, flouncing away before she'd made her little speech. One woman clenched a stem in her teeth, defiantly flamenco-style. Another plucked petals and threw them in the air. They were so young but they were so very ugly.

Watching them cavort among the headstones, Toni realized who she was waiting for and that she had, in fact, actually been waiting, scanning the assembly first at the church and now at the cemetery. Where was Sophie's so-called boyfriend Cody? The one who had dropped her off that fateful morning. The one who, no doubt, had given her what killed her. Some pill perhaps. Something chopped into something else that went up her nose or in her arm. Dolores had told her Cody was older. He was someone's husband and lived in Del Mar. He'd met Sophie at the club where she danced. Toni could picture him. A white guy, old enough to be her father, as they say. The son of old Del Mar money slumming in the city. She knew the type. She'd seen them her whole life. And just then she saw him, leaning up against the fence next to another guy all duded up in Wstern wear: boots, hat, suede jacket with fringe. The cowboy was sort of cute but the man she pegged as Cody absolutely wasn't, though he carried himself as though he was or once had been. Pudgy, pale, close-cut blond curly hair already beginning its retreat. Unfortunate mustache. Nice enough clothes that were a little too tight for his pudge. He drank something out of a can wrapped in an insulated holder. Even from here she could tell it was beer. But before she could go to him, offer him a rose and— *do what? say what?*— a woman approached her, sincere searching eyes above a pert teal KN95 mask.

"I want to offer you my condolences," the woman said, offering her hand. "This is a time of such loss for many." She paused, then continued, "But that doesn't make it easier." Her clothes were pressed, starched gray and white linen. Her cropped head of hair was sleek and black.

"You are—?" Toni began. Aside from her sister, this was the only person here who spoke to her as if she knew who Toni was, as if she understood where they all were and why: a funeral for a very young woman who had been failed in so many ways by so many and who finally failed herself. Then Toni remembered. The nurse. Dolores had mentioned that a nurse wanted to come to the service. Imagine that. This obviously reasonable woman was certainly the nurse. There had been so many during those five hospital days. An older one had pulled her aside early on, asked her if the family had begun to "prepare" themselves. Each one donned their personal protective gear—respirator mask, eye shield, gloves, gown, booties—before entering Sophie's isolation room, the bed visible through a transparent wall, accessible through a sealed entryway, beyond which family members could keep vigil, masked and distant. This earnest one must be the young nurse Toni had watched comb Sophie's long black hair one afternoon, a gesture performed with a gentle professionalism using a powdery product carefully applied and then brushed out. The young woman was comatose, her small body wrapped in pale blue hospital garb, the ventilator clamped to the lower part of her face, her fairy-tale princess hair spread around her. Toni had been planning to head home that day but when the nurse started brushing out Sophie's hair, she stayed, watched, waiting to thank the nurse who must know, as Toni did, that there was no coming back from where Sophie was. But still the woman washed the hair, combed it, arranged it as she thought the girl would want, finally weaving it into a thick braid. Some final beauty.

"Thank you," Toni managed. She wanted to say more, but her throat was dry. She swallowed the words instead. She offered a rose.

"I'm Vicki. We met at the hospital. You're the aunt, right? The great-aunt? You must have been a *great* aunt to her." Beneath the mask, Vicki was smiling at her own play on words, part of her effort at consolation.

Toni wished the nurse wouldn't try so hard. No, she thought with an immediacy that shook her. I was not a great aunt. I gave up. I let Sophie go. I let Brenda go. I let my sister go. I let them all go.

"I was expecting the detective to be here." Vicki looked around. "You know, the one who came to the hospital. Nice guy."

The detective. Jameson. "Like the whiskey," Brenda had remarked with an indulgent smile, constitutionally unable to not come on to him, "my favorite." Brenda was always on the make, looking for a mark. A survival tactic. That afternoon during the family interview, Toni saw that Detective Jameson was going through the motions, checking the boxes. When Dolores asked him if he was going to find the people who had done this to her granddaughter, Jameson had nodded, said they were going to do their best. Dolores believed him because she needed to believe something. Toni knew better. She saw how the detective sized up the three of them and then dismissed them. His eyes had seen it all before. There was no solving this case. No reason to. Not a priority. Who cared? No, Toni thought, Nurse Vicki can think that, but Detective Jameson was not a nice guy. But then again, could she blame him? What could he have done? Arrested them all? Where to start? Where to end? She herself had done no better than Jameson. She saw Vicki staring at a trio who had perched themselves like grinning gargoyles on a nearby stone bench that overlooked someone's loved one, passing a cigarette between them, swaying to some song only they could hear.

"I think the police hit a dead end," Toni said, just to say something, anything. "Fentanyl. It's an epidemic." At least that was true.

"Well, take care of yourself, and," Vicki's voice changed, "do what you can for the mother." Her eyes slid away to Brenda, who was facing off with the bishop at the white casket. The bishop's crisp blue business suit was beginning to wilt in the heat. It had been a long day. He wanted to get things started. Brenda didn't. They could hear her shriek from where they stood. Everyone could. High as a kite. A howl: "She was *my* bitch, not yours."

Toni was beginning to understand Brenda, the problems she, they, all faced. Then and now. No one knew what to do, what to fix first and how, or even if anything could be done, anything at all. So they'd done nothing. For years. Now this.

"Watch your sister, too. She's taking it hard. In fact," and Vicki began to move away, alert with nurse-like purpose, her rose in hand, "I'm going to go talk to her."

Toni watched as Vicki made her way through the small crowd and greeted Dolores with a smile and a hug. She knelt down in the grass beside her, holding both her hands in her own, the rose now on Dolores's lap. Dolores looked at Vicki as if she had been given a great gift. Nobody had been talking to her. Ray and his new wife were already on their way back to Barstow. The old, old friends had eaten their box lunches and gone home. Not every mourner makes it to the graveside. Some only show up for the lunch. And to the Laytons, who had come so far in their modest dresses and suits and found room for her in their rental car, Dolores was a lost cause. They had long blamed her for Brenda, for Sophie, for Jaco, for their boy Gideon who could have done much better. After this, they'd never see her again, in this life or in the one that waited for them in their exclusive galaxies. They spoke only to each other. Meanwhile, Vicki, a stranger, consoled her.

Toni had been standing in one spot for so long, she had begun to crush the grass beneath her feet into mud. The roses, she noticed, were beginning to droop, as if their stems were suddenly too thin for the blooms. She hefted what was left from the bucket, letting the water drip down her front. She knew she shouldn't, but damn if the water didn't feel good, cooling. She must have three or four dozen flowers piled high in her arms. She wanted only to be rid of them. She was done, so done. Someone somewhere, no doubt underpaid, had peeled the stems of most of their thorns and leaves, but still the leggy stems scratched and poked. The raft of roses was difficult, awkward to carry. She ended up hoisting the flowers like a large lazy baby, one almost ready to walk but still wanting to be held. She circled around the small crowd, making her way toward the cowboy, to the man she believed to be Cody. She saw that he and some others had found shade and a low cinderblock wall on which to sit. They had made themselves comfortable.

"You got something for us, sweetheart?" asked the cowboy as she neared with her dripping bouquet. Both men laughed, a little nervously, a little recklessly. She smelled the booze, the cigarettes. Afternoon drunks. Their smiles were leers. She understood that they couldn't help it. That's just what their mouths did.

Toni started her speech: "The family would like you to have a rose to remember—" but stopped and began again. The nurse's speech was better. "I want to offer you my condolences. This is a time of such loss for many, but that doesn't make it easier." She tried to meet their eyes behind their sunglasses. They were there somewhere. They had to be. These two men had known Sophie in unimaginable ways and surely carried that knowledge with them.

"And who are you?" she asked the cowboy.

"Luke."

"Here you go, Luke. To remember Sophie by." She took her time, examining the sheaf of roses before plucking one and presenting it.

Luke received his single rose, holding it pinched between thumb and forefinger, uncertain. He began to roll the stem between his fingers.

"And you? You are?" Toni turned to the boyfriend. She felt so certain of this too. It had to be him. It just had to. The roses began to slip from her grasp. She held them tighter. She could feel water leaking down her arms, her bare legs. Once she would have cared about such things, but not now.

"Cody." He sipped his beer. The more she looked at him, the older, the puffier he seemed. He was not at all pleasant to look at. What did he have that Sophie had wanted, needed? Money? Sex? Drugs? Attention? All of the above?

"Of course you are," Toni said. She made her voice loud, excited. "Cody! I've heard so much about you, Cody. These are for you." She nodded down toward the roses, the unopened buds lolling on their thin stems, the huge bouquet that needed her two arms just to remain intact.

"I know Sophie would want you to have these lovely rosebuds to remember her by, Cody. All of them. You're not going to have difficulty remembering Sophie, are you, Cody?"

Then she didn't so much give him the roses as thrust them

upon him. His arms opened. These were what was left, stems still dripping with water, the tight white tender buds still waiting to open. He staggered a bit, and the flowers began to fall.

"Let me help you," Toni said, adjusting his arms to better embrace the flowers. He was remarkably compliant or perhaps just intoxicated.

"You really need to use both your hands," she advised. She swiped the beer he still clutched. The insulated cuff around the can was made of black foam so thick that the impressions of his big fingers remained. She turned the can upside down and watched what was left pour into the grass. A thin yellow stream. Weren't you supposed to do that? Offer a libation to the dead? She let the can drop.

Cowboy Luke giggled and wiggled his single rose.

"Is something funny, Luke?" Her voice was beginning to sound like Jaco's, flat and toneless, too loud. Her thin black dress was sopping now, wet with flower water and her body's own waves of deep sweat from the day's endless heat. Without the shield of flowers, the dress clung to her body in ways that might amuse some, might attract men like these, this clinging second darker skin. If she could see her curves, her bulges, so could they. She thought of Sophie, Sophie's young body, her beauty, which these two and others had imagined was theirs.

Luke stopped giggling.

Cody began to squat down, as if to unload the roses on the ground, that carefully trimmed green cemetery grass.

"Don't you dare!" Toni cried, again in that loud voice that came from her gut, a flat roar. She used his name: "Cody! No! Cody, you must hold them!" she commanded. "Those are yours now. They are all that's left."

Her words had created a silence around them that made everyone look in their direction. What did they see?

Jaco ceased his stubborn orbit around Sophie's casket, a rose still clenched in each sweaty hand. Someone, his aunt, of all people, was shouting like he did, the bold language of demand and dismay.

Brenda, for once mercifully silent, reached for her son's hand.

The Laytons, Gideon included, stood impassive as usual, arrayed like a triumphant family portrait on a holiday card.

As for her weary sister Dolores, the poor woman looked frightened, approaching mortification, but then she perpetually looked like that, as if dreading what would happen next. And what happened next generally justified her fears and lately exceeded them. Maybe this time it would be different.

The nurse, Vicki, rose to her feet and stood behind Dolores's chair, her hands on Dolores's shoulders. Toni thought she saw her nod. Good. Good.

Julie Crawford, the funeral director who had seen it all, stood watching something entirely new. She reached for her cigarettes, then stopped. Her young sidekick stared.

Cody obeyed Toni. Just like that. He straightened. He stood. His leer disappeared. He held the roses as if waiting for a processional to begin.

Nobody watching this said anything.

Toni waited. She would wait until there was something more to say or someone who might say it. She had already said her piece. She could wait for the others, for as long as it took. After all, she had been waiting alone for a long time already. She suspected it would take a while for some to come to what she had finally found.

Visitors Together

The young man ahead of Yolanda in the visitor line for the psych ward carries two gifts: a large hardcover Bible and a selection of glossy underwire brassieres the color of gems found in a child's fairy-tale book: emerald green, ruby red, turquoise blue, a deep amethyst purple.

Yolanda wants to tell him that he'll never make it in with those bras, that the wires constitute a hazard, as risky as the drawstring cords she pulled out of the pair of now harmless sweatpants she has folded over her arm and readied for inspection along with, of all things, a showy red second-place award ribbon, an impulsive last-minute contribution from her daughter. She could also advise him how to slip the wires out: snip a hole near the top and then withdraw the flat metal crescents. She's done this before on her own bras, although for comfort, not security. The ward staff still might not approve. The shoulder straps could be dangerous, potentially fashioned into a noose, but then again, they might let them pass.

But Yolanda doesn't say anything. She can see the young man is upset. Though his skin is dark, his color is high like he's running a fever, his eyes red-rimmed. He is so deep inside himself that he isn't meeting anyone's eyes, unable to talk to anyone in the waiting room. She expects she will see him again at another visit, and then she can offer her old-hand advice about wires and cords, shoestrings and buttons.

The nurse approves his Bible, shrink-wrapped and beribboned, shakes her head at the brassieres. Yolanda could have also informed him that there were plenty of Bibles in there already, but she understands his need to bring something, anything. That's why she is standing here with sweatpants and a red show ribbon.

She watches as he returns to the bank of lockers where he has stowed his briefcase and coat to stash the bras. He struggles with the lock of the one assigned to him, looking down at the paper with the combination scrawled on it, then back up at the dial's round black-and-white face. The lockers are metal, painted white, like the kind found in high school gyms, with interior hooks to hang clothing and ventilation slats, as if one might also need for some reason to stash a small animal inside. The young man doesn't look as if high school was that long ago for him—five, six years at most. Still, the rotary combination lock resists him. He spins. He stops. He starts again, looking like he might cry.

"Let me help," Yolanda says, using that loud voice she developed over the years as a mid-level office manager, the indispensable person who makes things go. The job wasn't what she set out to do, but it was what she did. "I'm good with locks," she announces.

She leaves her place in line to join him. She is not surrendering much. It's midweek evening visiting hours at the psych ward. The line is short. They will all get in with plenty of time to spare. There is always plenty of time once one is inside. Yolanda's train home tonight departs at 9:30. The taxi ride will take fifteen minutes, twenty at most. The last train is always on time. It connects with the Coast Starlight in L.A. and travels all the way up to Seattle. Yolanda has never been to Seattle. She could be there in two days. Hospital visiting hours end at 9. It's just past 7 now.

He turns to face her.

"It's not easy," she reassures him. "I've just done it a lot." The combination's numbers are simple enough to read. She turns the dial to the right three times, then left, then right again. The lock falls open in her hand, heavy, cool.

The bras shimmer in his grasp, collapsed puddles of satin and lace.

"Pretty," she says, because she wants to say something.

"They won't let me," he replies.

"I know," she says.

A few minutes later, when she sees him sitting with his wife at a round table, the Bible still wrapped, gleaming under the fluorescents, she thinks that the woman might under other circumstances be just the type to appreciate the extravagant jewel-tone bras he brought, now confined in the metal locker. But here his beautiful young wife is swaddled like her fellow patients in soft forgiving clothing, the opposite of those bright binding foundation garments. Her breasts, full and no doubt lovely, are unimportant here.

Yolanda waits for her sister Ali to arrive. The staff has arranged full plastic water pitchers on each table. The cups are also plastic. No glass anywhere. She folds the sweatpants into a thick soft stack of gray. She places the red ribbon on top as if the pants have won some prize. Second place, to be precise. The streamers hang down. Festive.

The hospital doesn't call this the psych ward or, as her reliably jokester husband Brian is likely to privately quip, the loony bin. Those words, along with so many, have been retired, replaced with sincere, empathetic—if not entirely convincing—words. This is now the Behavioral Unit, nestled in a private hospital a few miles from the San Diego coast. The windows have bars, it's true, but they slide open, and on nights like this one you can smell the ocean, if not hear it over the sound of the cars below. The facility is lightly and tastefully decorated, painted in soft colors, like melted ice cream meant to calm even the people, like Yolanda, who are not patients.

Perhaps it's like a spa. Yolanda doesn't go to spas, doesn't believe in them, wouldn't know. Who has the time? "Remember," one of her co-workers advised her after Yolanda, in a moment of unguarded sharing while waiting for her single-serve coffee to brew in the lounge, had let drop her sister's latest mental health crisis, "remember to find the time for some self-care."

Self-care, yet another new term meant to make things seem better. Yolanda smiled as if receiving a gift that she knew was cheap to buy and easily given away. This was the same co-worker who had successfully lobbied behind her back to replace the old Mr. Coffee with its venerable twelve-cup glass carafe with a new coffee maker, one that brewed individual cups of different flavored coffees. Each single serving was finely ground and spiced and sealed in a tiny individual plastic tub whose foil top and plastic bottom were pierced by the machine, allowing the hot water to brew the beverage. As it was November, wintry seasonal flavors were available in a convenient stainless-steel stand: Pumpkin, Gingerbread, Peppermint Stick, Eggnog. Yolanda knew, just knew, that all the tiny plastic pods would end up in the Pacific Ocean one day, joining the floating garbage patch, three times the size of France, that stretched from the seafloor to the surface.

Yolanda had never been to France either and was beginning to think that she, like Lucy Jordan, heroine of the old Marianne

Faithfull song, would never ride through Paris in "a sports car with the warm wind in her hair." This year, Yolanda was now officially older than thirty-seven-year-old Lucy Jordan. She had sung that song as a punk dirge in her high school talent show, accompanied by her then-boyfriend banging on keyboards. They were so serious it embarrassed her now to think about it, two teenage kids howling about a suicidal middle-aged matron. Their duo hadn't won a thing that night, although her English teacher sidled up to her afterward and remarked, "Well, that was certainly brave."

Yolanda had learned about the garbage patch three times the size of France from her precocious daughter Alexandra, who would never make the mistakes Yolanda had in school. For the middle school science fair, thirteen-year-old Alex had constructed a facsimile of the Great Pacific Garbage Patch, working for weeks in the garage, weaving a translucent cloud of fishing line and trash that hung from the rafters, a mobile nearly as big as their tiny electric Fiat. It was punctuated with old toothbrushes, disposable razors, hair clips, plastic cutlery and plastic bottles, clamshell food containers, plastic pens, yogurt cups. Alex had scoured their own trash bins and the neighborhood recycling dumpster. With her father Brian, she'd gone to the beach and raked the tideline searching for authenticity in the flotsam, finding broken sand toys, fishing tackle, and one very ecstatic Barbie, stripped of clothes, blue eye shadow intact, blond hair wild with tiny, desiccated sea creatures. She'd strung the empty coffee pods Yolanda pilfered from work like popcorn strands for a Christmas tree. Her final touches were the twinkling lights she threaded through the mass and the neighbor boy's discarded tiny soldiers sewn to the edges. Deserters, Yolanda called them. Casualties, Alex corrected—they're dead, after all. KIA.

Alex took second prize in the fair. Her garbage patch, suspended from the classroom ceiling by a single strand of scavenged monofilament line, sparkling like an apocalyptic disco ball, was clearly the irresistible showstopper. But in the end, after the judges lauded Alex for successfully and dramatically demonstrating her chosen problem, they then faulted her for failing to propose an effective solution. The blue ribbon and the $500 scholarship were awarded instead to the student designer of the "Safe Swim Filter," a contraption that presumably solved somebody's idea of the pressing problem of long hair getting trapped in pool filters, the apparent cause of drowning in swimming pools and Jacuzzis worldwide. The girl's problem-solving filter included a blade that automatically cut long hair sucked into the filter, thus saving countless lives. Alex's solution was obvious, if impossible: reduce dependence on plastics and eventually cease their production. Below her floating garbage patch she provided a simple metal trash can filled with refillable water bottles as an object lesson. "Solution not practical," the judges wrote in their statement.

"You've been robbed," Brian declared as they left. "Not practical?" They stopped for tiramisu at the pricey Italian bistro to celebrate and commiserate. Afterward their collective breath made their tiny car smell creamy sweet with cocoa and coffee.

Alex slumped in the back seat inspecting her second-place red ribbon. "You know this was made by sweatshop labor," she complained.

"Irony!" quipped Brian. "That will kill us before plastic. Way, way before we get sucked under by a pool filter."

"I mean," said Alex, "it says so right on the tag. Made in China."

Yolanda liked that about her daughter. Alex got mad, not sad. She'd be just fine when she got wherever she was going.

Alex was certain to go places. Seattle. Paris. Hawaii. Beijing. Wherever she chose.

"Did they at least spell your name right?" Yolanda asked. Their hyphenated family name often suffered a variety of indignities. Alex had grown sensitive about this too.

"Unfortunately, yes. I don't even want this."

"Okay, okay. How about I share your ribbon with Aunt Ali when I see her tomorrow?" Alex had been named after her aunt, though both had abandoned the long, elegant Alexandra for shorter versions they believed fit them better.

"Please do. Tell her she can keep it." Alex tossed the ribbon up front, where it hit the windshield, then landed on the dashboard.

Brian grabbed it. "I'm a winner!"

"Both hands on the wheel, Dad," Alex admonished. "Please."

The science fair story pleases Aunt Ali more than Yolanda thought it would. But maybe it's just the gift of the ribbon, large and shiny, adorned with her niece's full name—Ali's own—in gold, plus the addition of Brian's last name, bridged with a hyphen: Alexandra Fonseca-Bergantz.

"I can keep it?" Ali asks, as if the ribbon's value were enormous. She looks better than she sounds on the phone. Someone has combed her graying hair and tied it back in a loose braid that appears almost chic. She has bathed. And even though her gaze often falls to the table, this Ali meets her sister's eyes when they speak. Best of all, she is drinking the water Yolanda has poured into the squat plastic tumbler. Small sips, but sips anyway. Two weeks earlier Ali had stopped eating and drinking, unable to swallow, though nothing physical was impeding her. It was, as it always is, in Ali's mind. Yolanda is glad she came to witness this progress, even though she suspects that Ali is just summoning up what courage she can for the visit. She is performing her recovery.

"Yes, it's all yours. Alex is so sorry you had to miss the fair." The events in Alex's short life that her aunt has missed are many. Better to recall the few times her only aunt made it up the 405: to watch a birthday cake be cut (but then decline to eat any) or to sit in an audience and wait for Alex's name to be called. But the science fair, featuring such terrifying global environmental and safety problems, would have unnerved her sister, Alex's mass of twinkling, gently gyrating trash most of all.

Yolanda looks over at the young couple. One of them has unwrapped the Bible. Its thin purple ribbon has fallen to the floor along with the balled-up shrink-wrap. Yolanda can already see the crumpled cellophane sphere floating out to sea, south first, bouncing off Baja's tip, then swirling up and over to the patch that floats between the Pacific coast and Hawaii, where the Bible wrap will find its final resting place. Yolanda has never been to Hawaii either.

Meanwhile, the husband has opened the Good Book and is reading to his wife. His voice started out soft but has grown louder, as if to capture her attention. Everyone in the room can hear him now: Yolanda and Ali, the middle-aged couple who have come to visit their tattooed son, the two daughters visiting their father, each group sitting at their own round island-like table. His young wife isn't looking at him, but instead has pulled their plastic pitcher of water close to her. She peers into it intently, her blank, beautiful face angled so it almost touches the rim, as if to see if it would fit.

Her husband is deep in Psalms, the only part of the Bible Yolanda still remembers from her childhood, when their grandmother gave both girls Bibles inscribed with their names. She doesn't know where hers went but she remembers the words of this psalm. Of course she does. Ali must too. It's the famous one about the shepherd, the green pastures, the still waters, and the valley. Yolanda sees her sister listening, watches the once-lovely face, so much like her own, grow wise in recognition.

"My cup runneth over!" Ali screams when the young man reaches that line. Her voice is suddenly full-throated. She is, after all, a former West High song queen. Ali's mouth breaks into a surprised smile. Everyone looks at her now. Ali lifts her plastic tumbler in a gesture of toasting toward the husband, then toward all the other tables. He stares. His wife remains entirely engrossed in the contents of the water pitcher.

Ali takes the tiniest sip and swallows. She smacks her lips. She holds up the red ribbon as if she has won it. Someone applauds. Yolanda doesn't turn around to see who.

In recent years Ali has become a regular in the Behavioral Unit, and last week she knew enough to check herself in when things started going wrong. She has a strong attachment to the private hospital with "mercy" in its name. This was where she had lost her only pregnancy, an early miscarriage with complications. This was where she had lost other parts of her insides. She doesn't blame the hospital. She feels safe there. In good hands, she says. Ali likes that word *mercy*. It was, she likes to say, going to be her child's name. Mercy. The insurance in the settlement provided by her ex-husband still covers her care.

And over the years and visits, Yolanda has learned how best to get there from the suburban office park where she works. It's a short drive to the train station, where she joins the commuters. As she isn't driving home until hours later, she can indulge in a cold beer (sometimes two) and a serviceable sandwich while watching the sun set from the Club Car as the train hugs the coastline south. A simple solitary pleasure. She never tires of that coastal stretch, the curling blue breakers, the surfers waiting for the right break, fishermen casting from the shore. Upon arrival at the depot, a waiting taxi ferries her inland to the hospital.

The first couple times, securing a taxi back to the train proved tricky. While the depot always had taxis lined up out front, for the return trip Yolanda had to call and wait at the hospital. As she was taking the last train north for the night, she couldn't risk being late.

One night Zemari picked her up at the depot in his big yellow taxi. Zemari was from Afghanistan. A widower with three teenage kids, he was talking to one of them on his cell phone when Yolanda climbed into the roomy backseat. Yelling, really. Shouting. Roaring.

"Zamir! Don't fight with your brother over television. So stupid. Be better. I have customer now."

He turned around in his seat and his voice fell to a polite softness. His big head filled the space between the seat back and the roof "You have kids?"

"One."

"Then you understand. Maybe. I have three. Where to, ma'am?"

He started driving to the hospital and, for whatever reason, perhaps the second Dos Equis, Yolanda found herself telling him that her sister was there and was very sick.

His gregarious taxi driver smile sobered. "Cancer?" he asked and without waiting for an answer told her about his wife, dead from cancer now for six years. "A terrible thing, cancer. Your sister, does she have kids?"

By the time they reached the hospital Zemari knew more about Yolanda than many of her co-workers did. Yolanda learned he had three boys, Zamir, Faisal, and Farzad. They were enshrined in framed photos on the dashboard. Three smiling boys who looked so alike they could be the same child at different stages of life. "We would have had more," he told her. "And you, do you want more kids?"

She saw him looking at her left hand. She and Brian weren't like that. No rings. No big wedding. This sometimes caused confusion for others. She shook her head.

"Your husband is a fool to risk losing someone like you!" He gave her his card. "Call me and I pick you up. Take you back to the train. Better than Uber."

Remembering the glance at her hand, Yolanda almost didn't call but then she did. It was late and she was two beers tired and Zemari was there, just like that.

This time when she crawled into the back seat, he was on the phone with his sister in Kabul. Kabul! Yolanda imagined the sister holding her cell phone to her ear talking to her brother, so far away in a city she would probably never visit. Yolanda, of course, didn't understand what they were saying but she liked the way Zemari sounded speaking to her.

"Somaya, my young sister," he explained, pulling away from the curb. "She is alone with her kids, like me with mine. I call her every day." When he dropped Yolanda off, he advised her to wait inside, close to the ticket counter. "Be safe," he said.

The next time she came south, she called Zemari from the train. "Remember me?" she asked.

"You are unforgettable pretty lady," he said. "How is your sister?"

Eventually Yolanda shared almost everything in those regular fifteen-minute conversations.

About Brian, her husband of fifteen years, wannabe stand-up comedian and proprietor of Off the Beaten Path bike shop.

"No rings? No wedding?" That Zemari didn't understand.

"A woman like you needs a ring, a big party."

About her sister's illness, not cancer.

"Worse than cancer, that!" he exclaimed. "It takes the mind."

They talked about their children.

"They are yours and then they are themselves," he said, shaking his head. "Watch out!"

They talked about their jobs. What they wanted to do, what they did instead. He wanted to be an engineer. Yolanda wanted to do something better with her sociology degree than administration.

The endless war in his country. Zemari had got out just in time. Her daughter Alex was born the year it started. Would it ever end? How? When?

His smoking. He stopped when his wife was dying but started up again after. Yolanda never started because her mother never stopped.

Yolanda likes that Zemari still calls her "ma'am" and "pretty lady" even though it goes against who she is, plus she knows she is not that pretty. Zemari must know that too. Maybe that's why he says it. Maybe that's why she likes it. Ali was the pretty one, everyone agreed. Yolanda was the smart one.

Tonight they are both tired.

Yolanda tells him about the young man who brought the Bible and the brassieres to his wife. She knows it will make Zemari laugh, and it does.

A Bible! Bras! Blasphemous.

"I helped him," she says, explaining that she had sat with the young husband in the waiting room afterward, slicing tiny slits in each cup with her Swiss Army knife and sliding out the potentially dangerous wires.

"That's why I was a little late tonight," she explains. Yolanda had sat there with the young husband as he passed one brassiere after another to her so she could perform the extractions. He was grateful, marveling at how quickly she worked. They were lovely garments indeed, finely made, not cheap. He handled them with such tenderness that Yolanda felt her eyes tearing up.

"See?" Yolanda pulls the wires out of her purse and fans them up so Zemari can see them in the rearview mirror. They are flat, curved like tired smiles.

"What are you going to do with those?" he asks.

"Take them home," she says. "Throw them away there." For some reason she couldn't toss them in the hospital trash can. No, she thinks to herself, better to tuck them into Alex's trash-cloud mobile. They will slide in smooth as fish hooks.

He laughs.

"You should have seen how happy he was," Yolanda says. "You know, he visits every day. He's going back tomorrow to bring her those bras."

"Good man," Zemari says.

Yolanda thinks about her sister. She is Ali's only visitor. Unlike the young husband, Yolanda has never visited every day or even every other day, though, she reassures herself, she calls most days. Most days. Not all. The days do go by.

"Have you ever been to Hawaii, Zemari?" she asks. In the map of the world that accompanied Alex's science project, the submerged hurricane of garbage hovered between this coast and those islands.

"No, ma'am."

"Me either. What about France? Paris?" How was it possible that the trash patch was three times the size of France?

"My wife, that's where she wanted to go one day, Paris. Very romantic. You, ma'am, do you want to go to France?"

They've been driving this same route for nearly three years now. Tonight he's taking surface streets because his phone told him about some accident on the freeway. They cruise past the vast darkness that is Balboa Park, the zoo. All those animals from other places sleeping, or, in the case of the nocturnal ones, not. That was the last place her sister and her daughter had seen each other. Four years ago? Five? Yolanda and Alex took the train down for the day. A different, less talky taxi driver delivered them to the park and deposited them by the big fountain. They had brought a picnic lunch to share near the big Moreton Bay fig tree. Her sister wouldn't eat the sandwiches they had cut in triangles, refused Alex's favorite potato chips, the bottled iced tea. Ali couldn't even bring herself to sit on the patterned sheet Yolanda had spread out on the grass. She stood and stood, smiled and smiled. Yolanda didn't think Alex had noticed but she worried she had. The kid was still so young. Eight? Nine? But even then, she paid attention. Alex ate all the spicy chips herself. Her sister left before they made it to the zoo, practically running away. After that, Yolanda stopped trying so hard. She just let her sister be.

"I think I'm *supposed* to want to go to Paris, to Hawaii, Seattle, to all those places," she tells Zemari.

"Yes," he says. "Americans, you go places." He laughs. They laugh together. The laughter revives them, and they are less tired now than they were.

When Zemari drops her off, he points inside to the waiting room as he always does, the long oak benches gleaming, a few other passengers waiting. "You are safer there," he says, as if he never said it before. "Till next time, pretty lady," he calls out, waving goodbye.

Yolanda watches as he parks in the short line at the taxi stand and pulls out his phone. She imagines he's calling Somaya, his sister. To see if she too is safe. Among other insights from her many rides with Zemari, Yolanda has learned that night in California is morning in Afghanistan. She remembers that when Zemari first told her he called his sister every day, she thought this was excessive, too much. Every day! Why? But she sees now he is like that young husband and his daily visits. Good men indeed.

The train depot is over one hundred years old. The classic Spanish Colonial style features twin white domed towers, archways, a red tile roof. Every time Yolanda walks inside, she thinks, *church*, even though there's no pulpit, just a ticket booth. She thinks, *history*. Inside the terminal, the ceiling vaults like a cathedral's, spanned by redwood beams and brass chandeliers and trimmed with walls of intricate blue, green, and yellow tile work. The stylized words "Santa Fe" sit in a tiled gold and blue cross as if trains are indeed worshipped here. The pew-like benches are deep and wooden. Yolanda reflexively admires it all. It's difficult not to. The station was built for the Expo over a century ago, like Balboa Park; it's as old as that big Moreton fig tree that shaded their uncomfortable picnic.

She took Alex down here that one time, that visit to the landmark park and the famous zoo with her solitary nervous aunt. It seemed like something a parent should do: take a child to a zoo to see the animals. At the time Alex was working on her fourth grade California mission project with a zeal that foreshadowed her Pacific Garbage Patch mobile. Disembarking from the train, Yolanda called Alex's attention to the station's architecture. She was doing that thing she did back then: performing parenthood whenever the opportunity presented itself.

"Oh, look, Alex! The tiles, the arches! Spanish Colonial. Isn't it pretty?" The tiles, yellow and blue and green, gleamed in the sunshine, edged in black with ziggurat patterns.

Alex roared back: "Do you know what the Spanish did to people, Mom? To people a lot like us?"

Yolanda didn't want to correct her daughter, didn't want to split genetic hairs, how much of them was one thing, how much another. Alex had cherished their bloodlines since learning, wide-eyed, that what made Mexican *Mexican* was indigenous ancestry. Of course Yolanda knew what the Spanish had done. But to hear it from her daughter was different, to be reminded of what she knew, not that she had much choice.

As they walked to the taxi stand, Alex let her have it, showing off all she had learned, in school and out, using the bold voice she must have inherited from her aunt, the song queen. Her mission project, a reconstruction of the celebrated one nearby in San Juan Capistrano, was faithful, not romantic. Using several Kleenex boxes and a decapitated bleach bottle for the centerpiece fountain, she fulfilled the assignment's basic requirements, producing an accurate representation of the mission, complete with tiny bells. But the child took it further, surrounding the mission with an unmarked burial ground that was equal in size, diminishing the mission's grandeur, with tiny graves cut into the elevated cardboard pizza box base that could be opened to reveal plastic dime-store Indians playing dead. The dead Indians were made of red plastic. Of course they were. The subtitle on the poster that explained her project read: *California's Missions Are California's Plantations*. Alex's outrage was so fresh. Her mother loved it, even when, increasingly, Yolanda herself was its target. Brian reassured her that this was to be expected, all a part of parenting.

Clearly it was past time to bring Alex down here again. She was no longer a child to be protected, if indeed that was what Yolanda had been doing all these years. She was the one who would grow up to go places, after all. Better start now. Here. They could be visitors together, eating sandwiches in the Club Car, no doubt pre-wrapped in nonbiodegradable plastic, walking through the problematically beautiful train depot, reading the historical marker and wailing about what was left out.

Alex could meet Zemari. He would like that. Alex would love him. She would have so many questions. Too many, perhaps. It wouldn't matter. Zemari would offer passionate answers, gruff blunt opinions. He always did. Zemari could drive them both together to the hospital, taking the scenic route to show off a bit of the town to Alex, who wouldn't remember all that much from earlier visits.

They could ride the elevator both together to the Behavioral Unit on the fourth floor, where they would stow their belongings in a locker and wait in line to be searched. They would wait for Aunt Ali to arrive in her new loose sweatpants, her hair softly braided. Yolanda would pour water for all three of them. Tap water out of a plastic pitcher into plastic tumblers. They would make conversation. And when visiting hours were over, they would together retrace their steps back to the hospital entrance. Zemari would be waiting in his big yellow taxi to take them back to the train that would take them home.

Alex could see for herself what good could be done for people, by people, to people and what, finally, perhaps could not. Anybody might see.

"Cielito Lindo"

When the twelve-piece mariachi band her uncle had booked to serenade his wife on their fiftieth wedding anniversary started playing, filling the church's basement room with the blast of five trumpets, Linda decided to sit next to her father after all because she knew they wouldn't be able to speak over the music and so she would get credit—good-daughter credit, she imagined—but at the same time she wouldn't have to say a thing or listen to what he had to say about her mother (*after all these years still "that crazy woman" if he were sober or "that bitch" if he were drunk*) or her own sorry life (*manless, childless, pointless in his view*). Linda also imagined that if she, his nearly fifty-year-old daughter, sat next to him, her presence might dissuade him from hitting on the younger female guests. She'd already seen his eyes wander as the generation of family grandchildren, now in their late twenties and early thirties, arrived, accompanied by their friends. The women wore dancing dresses cut just low enough to raise his hopes. He was drinking tonight, she noted, something dark and on the rocks.

Her father was handsome in a kind of craggy rooster-like way. He'd aged well and he knew it. Still had all his hair, more than most men forty years younger. Tonight he was dressed up in dark jeans and cowboy boots, a fine white shirt unbuttoned to show a puff of chest hair that belied his seventy-plus years. He always did that with his shirts and it embarrassed her, the sight of that patch of burnished skin and curling white hair. Linda wondered if, had she been a boy, the son her mother claimed he always wanted, she would now feel different, feel pride, a kind of male camaraderie rooted in perhaps her own hopes as a middle-aged male swimming in the same hairy gene pool.

Linda sat and watched her father move in rather gentlemanly appreciation of the music, his head nodding, his eyes beaming. It was as if he and not his brother-in-law had paid for the band and made the arrangements, displaying a kind of easy but dishonest sense of proprietorship that she often saw him deploy at family dinners and parties. As if he, along with the other tíos and tías, had helped out or pitched in when, as she well knew, all he'd done—again—was show up.

When the mariachis launched into the inevitable "Cielito Lindo," her aunt and uncle stood in front of the musicians. They swayed together, which was as close as they would ever get to dancing, and the crowd began to stand up too, singing along to the music they had heard their whole lives, in restaurants and on street corners, in movie houses and on car radios. It meant something to them all, if perhaps not the same thing, this song with its *ay ay ay ay*, with its command to sing and not cry. Some people, Linda noticed, knew all the words, and some knew only the chorus. Linda was one of the chorus singers.

Her father drained his glass, got to his feet, and began to sway, to sing. He knew all the words. He even turned to Linda and smiled as if she too, his daughter, was a lovely woman, worthy of such a song. Her father knew how to look at a woman and make her feel like that, she thought. Pretty. It didn't take much. Something about the full attention of his eyes. He bent down and reached out his hand, the gentleman again, a gallant gesture, to raise her to her feet. And when he did, when her old father leaned toward her, she noticed that his white dress shirt was undone one button more than his usual two. And when Linda stood beside him and glanced again, she saw that instead of his usual wife beater undershirt (*How she hated that name, however true it might be for him*) with its white ribbing and scoop neck, it appeared to her that her father was wearing a white camisole with a bouquet of embroidered flowers at its center. She looked away. Linda herself had worn such things as a girl, to dances in this very basement and yes, like her father, had left her blouses unbuttoned to the flowers, hoping perhaps that something else would show as well and that someone else would notice.

Linda watched as the bows of the violins cut the air with a kind of violence but, unable to help herself, her eyes shifted back to the garland of tightly stitched pink rosebuds with their satin petals and green leaves that adorned her father, his puff of chest hair rising now like a cloud above a garden.

Linda wondered what this girl's undershirt meant, with its tiny flowers: *Where did it come from? Whose was it? Had her father picked it up off the floor of some woman's bedroom, mistaking it for his own? Had he donned it like a strange trophy? Had the shirt made its way into his laundry at his apartment building and gone unnoticed? Did he know? Should she tell him?*

Her father was singing full-throated now, and when she looked at him in profile, Linda saw his strength and handsomeness, perhaps what her mother had seen, yes, over fifty years ago. But she also saw all those years gone and she knew there were not that many left for him now. Linda could see what her father could not: those flowers, that white hair, the mistakes a person makes.

Manuel

Years later, Manuel Estrada would own only sports cars, two-seaters so well taken care of that when he'd arrive at some family function, late as always, parking for an easy quick exit, the nephews and nieces crowded around, vying for rides or a look at the engine, for some car talk. Every decade seemed to feature a new car. In the sixties, when he split with Wife #1, the powder-blue Ford Thunderbird appeared. Then, after the second marriage broke up in the seventies, the sea-green Karmann Ghia sports coupe. The eighties brought the third and final divorce and a Chevy Corvette that would see him out. Silver, like his hair, a full head until the end, rolling back from his brow in a glossy static Brylcreem wave.

But in February 1948, almost two years after his honorable discharge from the navy and nearly three years after the end of World War II, here was Manny still riding his sturdy high school bicycle through the streets of South Central Los Angeles. The Schwinn he rebuilt from parts. He was twenty-one. Tonight he was headed toward the city, down Florence and a left on Central. Four miles to Second Baptist, the Negro church where Paul Robeson was to speak.

Three years earlier he'd been on the USS *Midway* during its maiden deployment in the North Atlantic, a teenage gunner's mate third class waiting for the war to grow in ways it never did. He would spend the rest of his life explaining to people that *Midway* the ship was *not* at the battle of Midway, but rather named *after* it. Sometimes he just gave up and passively accepted the accolades for a decisive battle fought when he was still sixteen and reading *The Red Badge of Courage* in English 101 at John C. Fremont High School. What people knew and what they didn't want to know. Manny was paired with a gunner named Henry Pruette, a good old boy from North Carolina who said he had never met a Mexican before.

"You still haven't," he told Henry. "If I was Mexican, I wouldn't be here." They wore matching dark blue navy-issue peacoats, their names and numbers stenciled inside in white, double-breasted with buttons embossed with ships.

Pruette was older by a couple of years. Unlike some on the ship, he seemed to want to make friends among the crew, which brought together men from all over, country boys like Henry and kids like Manny who'd never even left the cities they were born in until they shipped out. The pair got along well enough, sharing a penchant for the Westerns broadcast on Armed Forces Radio and hiding, as best they could, the shame of their seasickness.

Manny's two older brothers, drafted army privates, saw action in Italy where their California Spanish quickly made them Italian friends. Their brother didn't have the same opportunities to meet people. Manny saw the North Atlantic, endless dark waves like the gray silhouettes of the San Gabriel Mountains, Greenland with its monumental cliffs of ice, and once, with Henry on a few days of shore leave, New York City, which managed to make them feel smaller than the ocean had done. Too many people all at once. He saw the actor Gene Kelly too, in boot camp in Virginia. While the sailors made a circle around him and clapped, Lieutenant Kelly leapt into that famous Russian squat dance, the *prisyádka*. His alternating legs kicking out straight, his arms like wings, folding and unfolding, his sensitive narrow face, chin up, sweaty with joy. All that effort and exertion were somehow invisible beneath the exuberant dance. Manny had never seen anything like it, a bit of movie magic off the screen and here in front of him in a chilly airplane hanger, a man dancing to music that only he could hear but somehow, by doing so, his powerful legs shooting out, his eyes delightedly meeting the onlookers', Kelly made him hear the folksy martial tune of the nation that was then still our loyal ally in the great struggle. The music was familiar from newsreels and radio, rousing ideas in Manny's head that had rooted there in his youth when for a while he hawked newspapers on corners and dropped stacks at the local stores. He read the papers too. Better to sell them. That's where he first saw the name Gene Kelly. His two sisters loved musicals and they all rode the Red Car downtown to see *For Me and My Gal* at the Million Dollar Theater on Broadway. In the papers he read about the Zoot Suit Riots across town, learned about the Negro leaders who came to the city. In the newspapers was where the war at home and the one abroad became real. It was all there.

Manny's angry, widowed father never asked him where he was going. So Manny just went. In his ninth decade Manny would recall for anyone who would listen—and even those who didn't care to—that he had never had a conversation with the man, his own father, not a one. After the war, the family home, a three-bedroom house on East Seventy-Fifth, still seemed crowded despite the premature death of his mother and the postwar marriages of his brothers. Now it was just the old man and the two sisters and Manny. The two girls took care of the old man, and Manny, well, Manny took care of himself, finishing high school in night classes, enrolling in barber school and looking for something, anything better than he had and certainly better than his father, who dug ditches to lay cable for telephones. His father's days were dirt.

Henry Pruette wrote him letters complaining about North Carolina. He was thinking of reenlisting. He reminded Manny that he had a sister. Joanie. And recalled that he, Henry, had shown Manny photos of her and that Manny had agreed she was good-looking. She was. Henry said Joanie wanted to get off the farm, liked the idea of California, its oranges and palm trees, its movie stars.

Joanie wrote a letter too. It included three pictures cut from a photo booth strip showing a smiling blond with soft victory roll curls framing her cheerful face. He had never received mail from a girl before, let alone photos that fell from the envelope onto the Formica kitchen table. His sisters were curious, impressed by his blond admirer. He slipped the photos into the so-far-empty photo sleeves of his wallet just to make them disappear from his sisters' teasing. Joanie wrote that Henry had told her that he, Manny, knew Gene Kelly. She adored Gene Kelly, didn't believe what people said about him and his love for the Blacks. Had Manny seen *Anchors Aweigh* yet? she asked. Kelly and Sinatra reminded her of him and Henry. The film made her want to visit California even more. She signed it "Affectionately."

Fifty blocks to the church. Like most L.A. city streets, Central Avenue ran straight and flat, just fine for his single-speed bike. The four-lane avenue was quiet this Monday evening. The jazz clubs, the ones that made this strip of the city seem like what he and Henry had glimpsed in Manhattan were closed: Club Alabam, the Downbeat, the three-story Elks Temple. It was a cold night, no rain yet but it could happen. Gray clouds had piled up and tumbled over the Santa Monica mountain ridge all afternoon, promising something. He left the navy peacoat unbuttoned as he pedaled, keeping close to the curb, watching the numbers grow smaller on the street signs. The blocks weren't that long. Ten strides on the bike if there weren't any interruptions, an idling car, a long red light.

He'd first seen the ad for Robeson's appearance in the *California Eagle,* the local Negro-owned newspaper he used to sell. Then the handbills appeared posted on telephone poles. He'd recognized the name. His high school history teacher had played Robeson's "Ballad for Americans" one afternoon, cuing up the phonograph and extracting the thick 78 from its sleeve with care. It was, Mr. Kovner announced, the history of the country in song. Some students groaned. In Manny's memory, the song filled the entire class hour, but when he heard it years later on Armed Forces Radio in the middle of the Atlantic, it lasted only ten minutes. The rest of that class must have been the teacher holding forth on Robeson: the gifted student who helped break the color barrier at Rutgers, becoming valedictorian and named All-American in football, then Columbia Law School, then some years with the NFL and then, with his bass-baritone voice, a groundbreaking career in theater and song. It all seemed so unlikely: football, law, music, theater.

Now the singer his teacher loved was here. Last night Robeson had appeared at the Shrine Auditorium, and tonight he would be at Second Baptist. The Shrine performance was a fundraiser that required purchase of tickets, but the church event was free and, as the fliers proclaimed, "Open to the Public." At twenty-one, Manny felt he was finally part of the public, a veteran, a barber-in-training, the recipient of letters via the U.S. Post Office, a reader of newspapers and posters, an American.

Second Baptist stood tidily on a corner, all pale pink brick with white detailing, the soaring square bell tower topped by a cross. Tonight its arched windows blazed with light. People streamed by on the sidewalks outside. Manny stashed his bike in some nearby bushes and jogged toward the church, joining the crowd.

The last time he had been in a church was for his mother's funeral Mass in '42. Saint Raphael was the small one she'd walked to, head covered with a simple chapel veil, her well-washed children in tow and, on special occasions—or when, Manny suspected, he had sinned in some way—her husband too. Father O'Toole presided, his Irish-inflected tongue making the Latin Mass musical to Manny's ears, if still unintelligible. Her own funeral service had been merely dutiful, poorly attended. There was a war on. So much loss elsewhere. Her two oldest sons were newly deployed. Most of her people were still in Mexico. Still, the neighborhood showed up. Women like her, wives and mothers of the children who played with hers, shocked by her sudden departure, the swift massive heart attack. Church was something Manny did with and for his mother. With her gone, he never went back. It was not for him. Ritual and refrains comforted her but not her youngest son.

Now Manny made his way in with the slow-moving throng, up the remaining steps, squeezing through the double doors. The crowd wore their Sunday best on a Monday night. Women with hats and gloves, men in sharp suits. Hundreds made their way down the aisles and into the pews. Robeson, well over six feet, broad-shouldered, handsome, was easy to spot even in a sanctuary full of tall, broad-shouldered, handsome men. The flock parted around him. He was working the room, shaking hands, pausing for photos marked with the pop of flashbulbs. Manny slid into a pew in the back, joining what seemed to him to be a multi-generational family, two parents with two reluctant well-dressed teenagers along with at least one pair of grandparents. The thin bald man he pegged as Grandpa looked him over with a plain, direct gaze. Manny felt he met with his approval when the old man gave a little nod, sliding a bit closer to his granddaughter, to give him more room. Soon it would be standing room only.

After a pro forma series of welcomes by local notables, leaders in the trade unions, elected Negro officials, and a blessing from the Second Baptist's Reverend Holmes, Robeson assumed the pulpit. He was gracious. He thanked the CIO United Public Workers, the Civil Rights Congress, and the State, County, and Municipal Employees union. He made a joke about why he wasn't speaking at the First Baptist Church, why he was never asked to speak at any First Baptist churches. Manny didn't get it, but the crowd roared. Then he started in. The failure to enforce the Federal Fair Employment Act. The need to support anti-lynching legislation.

"Have any of you seen a Negro man lynched?" he asked, his voice booming them into silence. "Have any of you known a Negro man who was lynched?"

Voices responded affirmatively.

"Enough. *Enough!* We fought for freedom in Europe and we came home to lynching, to discrimination in the workplace, in housing, in education." Persuasive narratives were offered. Senator James Eastland was condemned. Robeson reminded them that they had friends in nearby Hollywood, mentioning a few names including Manny's fellow seaman Gene Kelly. "We are not alone," he declared. "Look who is here with us tonight! Our friends in solidarity, who came out this dark night to stand with us. Stand up, brothers and sisters! Stand up!"

Manny felt eyes upon him. He was a brother, it seemed. Grandpa nudged him and gave him yet another direct plain gaze. He stood. He thought he saw his old high school history teacher Mr. Kovner, a few rows ahead, rise to his feet. Of course he'd be here. The assembly applauded.

"Stay on your feet," Robeson instructed. He announced he would close by singing a song about an American martyr. John Brown, he said, stood up for what was right, as we all must.

If Robeson's speaking voice had filled the hall, his singing voice, entirely unaccompanied, reached the rafters and made them tremble. By the end of the first chorus of the ballad about the mad abolitionist, the entire assembly was standing, singing along as if all were marching out together into that night where, as they and Robeson sang, "the stars above in heaven now are looking kindly down." Manny had never felt anything like this before, not in school assemblies, not in the navy when the national anthem was played and they stood and saluted, certainly not in his mother's church. His bones. It was like that phrase about feeling things in your bones.

When the song was over he began to make his way out, though the crowd was slow to move and leave. While his father wouldn't be worried that he was out so late, his sisters certainly would be.

"Estrada!" The voice was familiar. "Manuel Estrada!"

He stopped on the church steps and turned back.

It *was* Mr. Kovner. A little older, a bit thinner in all ways, including his hair, which had paled and lost its manic curls. Manny was surprised the teacher remembered him. He had not been an exceptional student, though he hadn't been a terrible one either. Now here was his old teacher catching up to him in the cold night, exuberant after the speeches and song, reaching out to shake his hand, smiling broadly. "Manny! Where were you deployed? When did you get back?"

Mr. Kovner knew the difference between the battle of Midway and the carrier *Midway,* of course he did. He appreciated the Gene Kelly cameo, and offered his condolences about Manny's mother. "You were her youngest, yes?"

Manny nodded. All the Estrada children had had Kovner for U.S. history. The one time his mother visited the school, the teacher offered up a polite greeting in Spanish, said something nice about her hijo.

"And now?"

"American Barber School."

At this Kovner paused his encouraging head nodding. "Hmmm," he replied, "I never imagined you cutting heads."

Manny was surprised that Kovner imagined him doing anything at all. "Steady work," he offered. "A six-month course and then I get my license."

"Hmmm."

Kovner's hmmm's were never a good sign.

"Can I give you a lift?" his old teacher asked.

Manny shook his head, motioning away. "I got my bike."

"Of course you do. Well."

Their gazes drifted back to the doorway as Robeson emerged, framed in arched light, appearing not unlike those portraits of saints in Manny's mother's church.

"What a night," Kovner observed, reaching out to shake his hand again. "Drop by sometime. I'm in the same room. Good to see you here."

The ride home down Central went fast. It was slightly downhill, not that Manny had noticed the gentle incline earlier. But now with the streetlights glowing, a misty fog rolling in from the distant Pacific, and few cars, he seemed to glide. The rubber tires whispered on the damp pavement. As he glided, gaining speed, he felt as if he could predict which lights would stay green. It began to feel as if the lights would be green all the way down, one green light after another after another. Robeson's voice was still reverberating in him. Then he heard the siren and glimpsed the red flashing lights that meant he had to stop. He must.

He pulled up against a newsstand. Gary Jackson's. Jackson was from Boston. Manny first met him when he was a kid more interested in comics than newspapers. The job came later. He propped his bike against the closed metal door front and waited.

Two officers emerged from the cruiser, one named Brown, the other Nelson, according to their nameplates. They were not much older than him.

Manny smiled. At least he thought he did.

Officer Brown told him they had seen him at the Second Baptist and used some words to describe the church that Manny wished he hadn't heard. Officer Nelson used some choice words to describe Robeson, then asked for identification.

A car drove by. Manny hoped it might be Kovner, but it wasn't. The white driver shot him a sympathetic look, a wry smile, and kept driving. Manny reached inside his peacoat and retrieved his wallet.

"Navy?" Nelson asked, motioning to his coat, the white credentials stenciled inside.

"Yes, sir," Manny replied, summoning up the tone he used on board the ship with his superiors. Most everyone was his superior.

"Where?" asked Nelson. Suddenly the two police officers were more genuinely interested.

"On the *Midway*."

"Midway!" exclaimed Brown. They were both impressed and began to tell Manny all about the battle. The destruction of the

Yorktown and *Hammann*, the survival of the *Enterprise* and the *Hornet*. The loss. The luck.

Manny added a few authoritative details of his own.

"You look a little young for the Midway," Brown observed.

"I lied, sir, about my age," lied Manny. "I wanted to serve."

Officer Nelson opened the mostly empty wallet, examined the Fremont High School ID, the American Barber School enrollment card, and then lingered over the three newly installed photos of Joanie. He offered the wallet to Brown.

"This your girl?"

Brown made a crude remark about Joanie. Nelson laughed.

Manny thought about how to answer the question. Joanie was not his girl. He'd never had a girl, but if he did, he knew it wouldn't be Joanie. Still, he wanted to defend her from the officers' disrespect, not add to it. After all, what did she know on that North Carolina farm except that she wanted off it? What did she get in any school to teach her any different? Her brother got the war and the world but Joanie stayed on the farm. Now here she was in the hands of these two, being passed around like a cheap magazine. But before he could settle on a reply, Nelson returned the wallet. From inside their cruiser, the radio had squawked. The two police officers were suddenly bored with him, ready to move on. And they did, first offering some parting words about Robeson, about Joanie.

Manny remembered this encounter years later when his nephew Frankie, the firstborn of his eldest brother, the one who was supposed to become a priest but instead dropped out of seminary and enrolled at Berkeley, delivered his FBI file as an unexpected eighty-fifth birthday present.

Frankie was a political science professor at a public university, his special focus the study of hate and extremism. He had become one of those go-to experts pursued by reporters in the aftermath of atrocities. A talking head holding forth after church and synagogue bombings, after mass shootings at schools and shopping malls. Dr. Francisco Estrada. But first Frankie had been one of those nephews who admired Manny's fleet of sports cars. Later Frankie became more enamored of the tales he could pull out of the old man. The night Tío Manuel heard Paul Robeson speak at the church was one of his favorites.

Curious, he searched out his uncle's past and applied for what he suspected would be an FBI file using the Freedom of Information Act. After all, Paul Robeson had been under their surveillance since the early forties. The file that arrived via U.S. post was slim, but there it was—that one night, Second Baptist, Paul Robeson, the encounter with the police officers, the Fremont High history teacher Benjamin Kovner, who was described as a "premature anti-fascist," even a few mysterious redactions. Manny was delighted and sat in his recliner reading it as if it were a novel.

The FBI file no doubt partially explained why, when Manny applied to join the L.A. Fire Department in 1951, the honorably discharged World War II vet was initially rejected as "physically unfit." The graduate of American Barber School had indeed discovered that, while he enjoyed getting a good haircut and a nice shave, he couldn't imagine giving them for the rest of his life. With Kovner's encouragement, he set his sights on the fire department. Service. Camaraderie. What he had liked best about his time on the *Midway*. But years after that Federal Fair Employment Act Robeson had railed about, Manny still had to fight for the job. His father was discouraging: Ellos no te quieren. ¿Porque los quieres? *They don't want you. Why do you want them?*

It took years and an appeal, but Manuel Estrada became

one of the city's first Hispanic firefighters, not that the department used that word then. They used Henry Pruette's term. That was the job that let him buy his first car and all the ones that came after.

Years later when the task to clear out his apartment, what Manny liked to call his "bachelor hooch," fell to him, the favorite nephew, Frankie found the FBI file again. That first year of the pandemic had left his aging uncle, the sole survivor of his siblings, alone when he began to die and make decisions about how he would do so: sooner, not later. This was, he assured Frankie, how he wanted it. "It's like the tide going out," he said when Frankie finally found him in a hospital, refusing all measures that would extend his life but limit his independence.

His uncle was not a religious man, Frankie told the cheerful nondenominational Hawaiian shirt–wearing chaplain who showed up during one of his visits. Manny roused himself from his bed the best he could. Soon his death certificate would note that his tall frame had wasted down to 120 pounds. He was all bones, but his brown eyes were bright. "I dislike institutional religion," he told the chaplain, who sported a clear pandemic face shield, the better to smile. Manny was still angry about the church burning Joan of Arc at the stake. "Who would do that to such a beautiful girl so full of faith?" he asked.

The chaplain had no answer.

But he was spiritual, Manny insisted, and had morals that didn't come from a god or a book. Manny decided to tolerate the cheerful chaplain because he also was a chaplain in the fire department and a former navy man. So they had lots to talk about during the time that was left to him. The chaplain knew the difference between the battle of the Midway and the *Midway*. That was good enough.

On the cheerful chaplain's final visit, Manny was

nonresponsive. He lay in the hospital bed, eyes closed, mouth open, breath shallow. Frankie was playing music on his computer. Paul Robeson. Spirituals, as it happened: "Jacob's Ladder," "Swing Low, Sweet Chariot."

The chaplain offered to play the songs on his tubular Bluetooth speaker, which he produced from his backpack. "It will sound better," he advised.

Frankie agreed and spelled Robeson's name for him. He told him all about Paul Robeson. The singer was news to the chaplain. They also talked about John Newton, who had written "Amazing Grace," as they listened to Robeson sing it. The Bluetooth speaker did make Robeson's voice boom in the small room.

Among his uncle's papers, the stuff of life, vital and mundane, the FBI report, the Fremont High School diploma, the American Barber School license, three marriage certificates and three divorce decrees, decades of birthday cards from family and old flames, LAFD documents, faded handbills, coupons for car washes, and rubber-banded stacks of business cards, was a blank envelope containing three black-and-white photo strip portraits of a young blond girl, smiling hopefully at the camera. She sure was a looker. Frankie flipped the photos over, hoping for a name, but found none. In the envelope was the start of a letter on drugstore notepaper torn from a pad, a thin strip of adhesive gum still clinging to the top: *Dear Joanie,*

The Mayor and the Folksinger

The last thing the embattled Mayor needs is the famous lady Folksinger, sitting up in a tree.

But the tree-sitting musical legend is, apparently, the last thing—or damn close to it today, or tomorrow—which is why he finds himself driving alone across the city in the early morning hours. His Honor has perhaps just enough time to act before the police move in, supersized in riot gear like some kind of cartoon fighting force. Their dawn raid will target the defenseless Folksinger, armed only with her acoustic twelve-string guitar and her famous nonviolent convictions. There is time yet before the men with roaring chainsaws surround the tree and the TV cameras roll. The Mayor, sleepy, can't stop the cops but feels confident he will persuade Madame Folksinger. Years ago he listened to her LPs in his bedroom, kneeling beside the portable turntable that opened up out of a tiny blue suitcase. She'll have to listen to *him* now. He needs her.

The Mayor has decided against calling Javier, his driver, which would alert his security detail. Instead he's slunk out of the house wearing jeans and his teenage son's black hoodie, pulled up and over his head to hide his trademark hair, the dark wavy thickness of which once telegraphed vitality and youth to the voters. Silvery human skulls adorn the hoodie, cascading over each shoulder and spiraling down the arms. He's even put on his son's new shoes, $200 Nikes weirdly marketed as "retro huaraches," but which look more like the kind of protective footgear needed to walk on the moon or tread cautiously around a hazardous waste site. He still can't bring himself to call them sneakers. Two hundred bucks. Perfect, he thought when he saw them waiting obediently by the back kitchen door, their placement the evidence of household rules his wife had instituted since their arrival at the residence. No shoes inside the house. "No one," she retorted when their son complained, "is going to call us dirty Mexicans. Shoes *off*."

His son's beloved Camaro—1968, Rally Sport, primer gray, its guts torn out and rebuilt—starts right up and, as the Mayor backs out of the long driveway of the residence, he notes that no one, not security, not photographers, not lurking late-night media, follows. The dark empty street in the oval of the rearview mirror relieves him. If he is going to succeed, if he is going to get the Folksinger out of the tree, he has to go it alone.

Forty years earlier, when he was his son's age, he had himself worn the strange costume of that rare bird, the Mexican hippie: bell bottoms, fringed leather vest, beads, squeaky huarache sandals—real sandals, bought cheap at the swap meet—and smoky patchouli oil. He'd taped a poster of the Folksinger high on the wall over his teenage bed. She stood alone on a boulder by the blue Pacific, cradling her guitar, a foggy coastal pine forest rising beside her. He knew her bare feet, her downcast brown face, and that luminous smile—knew it as well as he knew his mother's smile or, yes, the Virgin's. It was that same singular smile that the best women in his life had given him at one time or another. That smile he works for still, the one he pledged to himself he would never betray.

He was sixteen, the hot asphalt of the city summer and his driver's license weeks away. His mother had promised him the keys to the old Plymouth in exchange for As and Bs on his report card. It was powder blue and laced with rust, but it was a car. She stood in the doorway to his room, tapping her foot, the same foot that worked the sewing machine at work and the gas and the brakes on the old car. She wasn't smiling.

Listening to the Folksinger, he explained to her, was like being at Mass, *except*—he searched for the difference.

Before he'd tacked up the poster, nothing had hung on his bedroom walls unless placed there by his mother: a few certificates from elementary school (*Good Citizen! Best Speller! Perfect Attendance!*) and a studio portrait of mother and son, taken shortly after his father had left. Hopeful evidence that the two of them were family enough. They smile in front of a generic woodland backdrop of his mother's choosing: fir trees, blue sky, fleecy clouds. Her hands clasp his shoulders like a pair of parentheses. He is eight, all crew cut and big front teeth.

Listening to the Folksinger's voice was like riding a cool pure river to heaven, thought the future Mayor, though he couldn't admit that to his mother. Even thinking it made him nervous, caused him to recall poems in English class. He had never even seen a real river except for the paved gutter next to the freeway. When it rained, it filled with churning water. Nothing cool about it, nothing pure. Junked cars and abandoned appliances floated in the tumbling dirty current. Kids who'd never seen it like that fell in and were carried away. Every year or so, one of them drowned and was memorialized at the water's edge in puddles of dripping candle wax, stuffed animals, and plastic flowers.

No, the Folksinger's soprano was nothing like that river. And *heaven*? A happy ending promised to people at the conclusion of lives spent kneeling in church and at work. But he couldn't tell his mother that either.

Her singing was like church, the boy-who-would-be-Mayor finally said, except no priests.

Church?

His mother winced. She stood framed by the hallway light, disapproval in her crossed arms, her deep judging silence. His mother was a different kind of body of water, he thought, the kind that never stopped moving, never dried up. She wasn't the Folksinger's cool mountain ride or the city's seasonal gutter flood. She was something else.

She knew it could have been worse. Her boy was a good boy. You might only look next door and see Rigo, Monica's boy, to understand what might happen to a kid in this country, growing up without a father in this city, in this time when girls took off more than their shoes and boys, *well.* Rigo was responsible for the pregnant fifteen-year-old who lived downstairs. They would get married soon enough, and though there would be a church wedding and a party in the apartment complex's courtyard, the future Mayor's mother knew the end of that particular story. Everyone did, though they pretended to believe something else was possible. Possible, but not likely. Yes, she could have worse problems than a poster of a braless barefoot guitar-playing girl who let her hair hang down like she didn't care.

The Mayor's mother didn't have to worry for long. When his friends saw the poster, their snickers, their disapproval, carried more weight than hers. *It's one thing to listen to her, ese,* his friends said. *It's another thing to put her on the wall. After all, this is the seventies and the folk scene is so, so sixties. Sure, she's fine, but she must una vieja by now. Think about it. Do the math, brother.* They drove him to the local record store where he'd bought her poster and let him choose her replacement, the pulsing beat of rock anthems percolating from the FM car radio.

So down came the barefoot Folksinger. She was briefly replaced with an ecstatic Carlos Santana crowned with a cosmic psychedelic halo, followed by a not-yet-iconic Che in his jaunty beret, a saintly Cesar on the march, then a stylized Ruben Salazar, and finally Zapata, his mustache broad as an eagle's wingspan, his sombrero even broader—a parade of men, fully clothed and shod; men in formidable attire; men, living and dead; men with ideas, guitars, guns, pens; men with armies and bands; men with other men standing behind them. When the Mayor finally left to go to the big university on the other side of the city—brick buildings, marble floors, windows that looked out onto the leafy trees, bright green sycamores, purple flowering jacarandas—he imagined he'd left the Folksinger behind in the dark closet, rolled up, secured with a rubber band that through the years must have dried out, frayed, then snapped.

But now she was back. Not hanging on his bedroom wall, not lying unfurled on the floor of his teenage closet, not headlining oldies shows at the famous amphitheater in the foothills, but sitting high in, of all places, a walnut tree in a blighted neighborhood, refusing to move. The Folksinger had answered the call and allowed herself to be hauled up the tree by ropes and pulleys. Tierra y libertad.

The Mayor had seen the same aerial photos everyone had: a square of dense verdant green erupting in the otherwise bleak city grid, not unlike how a scene in a pop-up book defies the predictable flat page. For over a decade, people cultivated the lot, doing what the desperate do when no one is using something as useful as land. And the land, as in one of those magical tales where ordinary beans grow into trees that climb to heaven, came back to life.

Then the cranky absentee owner appeared, like a stingy storybook monarch, to reassert his rights. What was now garden—*the largest urban farm in the country*, claimed its supporters—would be converted into a long-term self-storage business where people who had too much stuff could pay to store their excess and visit it on weekends.

And so the Folksinger stood on a platform nestled high in the tree's limbs and sang on the local news: "No nos moveran." All the old hits. "De colores." "Solidarity Forever." Her black hair had grayed but her large brown eyes and her brilliant smile were the same. The farmers, mostly working-class immigrants, gathered about the trunk of the great walnut tree and sang along. "*No, no, no nos moveran. No, no no nos moveran,*" they sang, "*Like a tree growing by the water, we shall not be moved.*" The unmovable singing farmers led the news night after night during this, the city's slow news season, with tragically few tragic celebrity deaths or sleazy political peccadilloes. Today the farmers' final appeal had been lost.

At times, the Mayor hears his life story via the Grand Biographer, the whispering narrator who has taken up residence in his head, the person who puts it all together, who sees where the Mayor has come from and predicts where he's going. The crafty and cool voice of one who sees his past and future in terms of chapters in a best-selling book, the Mayor's life like the arc of a rainbow: one end in the hood, the other behind the shining desk of power beneath the white dome of a civic building. Tonight the Grand Biographer rides shotgun in the Camaro, slouched down low, eyes alert, looking for the story. The Grand Biographer is so cool that sometimes the Mayor forgets he's there, the murmur of his familiar voice-over narration purring like a public television documentary turned down low.

He isn't a moony teenager any longer; he is the Mayor, serving one of the nation's largest cities and a leading, no, *the* leading Latino leader. But two years into his term, his lauded potential and shiny charisma are beginning to dull, to crack. It hadn't taken long. Resentment and hostility exploded from the predictable quarters: the ascendancy of a mayor whose parents were born south of the border was played as a threat. Those people questioned everything: his birth certificate, the sketchy residency status of his now long-dead mother, his father's disappearance. The affiliations and political causes of his youth were distorted, exaggerated to make him a traitor, a radical agent bent on returning the American Southwest to Mexico. Even the people on his side were forgetting his victories—*their victories*—didn't understand the position he found himself in, withdrawing their affection, suggested the Grand Biographer, like betrayed lovers pulling away blankets during a chilly night of confession. Inevitable corruption scandals and compromises-slash-sellouts tarnished his once glowing promise. Some seemed to be waiting, even eager, for his defeats.

Now the Folksinger in the tree and the lost urban garden make just two more items on a growing negative list in the newspapers. Even the Mayor's adjectives are changing, warns the Grand Biographer. He is no longer "pioneering," "visionary," "fearless" or, his own favorite, "Kennedy-esque." He is dangerously close to resembling his pudgy Anglo predecessor: "weak," "ineffective," "beleaguered," "embattled." That wasn't supposed to happen. Everyone knows he is meant to be governor in four years, senator in ten and then . . .

But maybe, just maybe, if the Mayor can get the Folksinger out of the tree, that would be something, like the night he negotiated the settlement of the longshoremen's strike, wading into the sit-in protest that had halted rush-hour traffic on the

Harbor Bridge, or the time he stood vigil at the burning ruins of an inner-city high school auditorium, refusing to leave until he'd raised enough money on the spot to ensure its swift reconstruction. An impromptu impassioned telethon that the cameras ate up. Pledges came pouring in. Yes, he thinks, he needs something like that, something he can sell. He needs the Folksinger to take his hand and climb out of that tree.

The night air is cool, but the city sidewalks are doing their alchemical thing, so that even in the early morning hours, the Mayor feels the heat of the summer day stored up, the smell of hot concrete mixed with asphalt, dust, and oil. He approaches an empty intersection and slides into the left-turn lane, waiting for the arrow. He waits as the signal lights up for first one direction, then the other, running through its short rainbow: green, yellow, red. The cycle begins again, but without ever flashing him a green arrow.

The Mayor backs up the Camaro, then drives forward, then back again, trying to trigger the motion sensor embedded beneath the asphalt. It is there somewhere. A little to the right, perhaps, maybe to the left. He's seen charts, diagrams. He knows how the city works. It is, after all, his city.

❦

The Mayor does his best thinking at night. Even as councilman and before, as a community organizer, a student, a young man with too much time on his hands cruising in that wheezing ancient powder-blue Plymouth. He loves driving around the city in the early hours. Lights smear the dark streets. At night the gum-pocked sidewalks, stained with spit and littered with trash, glitter; the tiny sparks of quartz and broken bottles catch the streetlights, the headlights of cars like his. Somehow, the sleeping city—the quieted streets, the absence of that pressing population that chokes it during the day—gives the Mayor ideas of what can be done. Awake and asleep, you need really to see the city both ways, he believes.

It took a while to get used to a chauffeur, just as it took Javier, his night driver, time to adjust to the Mayor's nervous insomnia, his desire to drive and just keep going until, sometimes, the eastern sky is brightened with the light of the rising sun, and then, instead of returning to the residence, they head toward City Hall where the Mayor keeps extra suits, changes of clothing. One night, not long after he took office, he directed Javier to drive by the old apartment building where he'd last lived with his mother. It was nearly 2 in the morning, but a trio of teenagers lingered, hanging out on the front stairs, smoking cigarettes. They stretched their lanky bodies down the steps, reclining on their elbows.

"Slow down," the Mayor had instructed. The kids noticed the slow crawl of the shiny town car and tensed, but not too much. They'd seen it all and this fancy car cruising the hood wasn't much. Not the cops. Not INS. Not ICE. Just a curiosity. The Mayor's impulse was to get out of the car and join them, make the pitch for an earlier bedtime and school, the usual pep talk, if perhaps delivered with more authority considering he could claim the place as home, could tell them a few things that would have proved it. He was, after all, El Homeboy Mayor. Say, he'd ask them, does the laundry room on the ground floor still make the second-floor units sweat? Who lives in number 8? Miss Monica's Rigo? Not likely. More likely Rigo's ex-wife and her grandbabies. Does the number 44 bus still keep the folks in front up all night?

"Used to live here," he told Javier.

"Better not, sir," Javier replied, as if the Mayor had asked a question. No doubt Javier got his own directives, and letting the

Mayor approach unidentified teenagers in violation of curfew was definitely not among them. Javier had his own job to think of, his family, his first wife in Riverside, his mortgage on a house in Paramount. This was the best job he'd ever had.

The kids didn't look dangerous, but then they never did, the Mayor thought. They just looked like who they were—kids growing up where no one wanted to be, not other kids, not adults. This made them do things that they shouldn't just to show that they could. Most of the time no one noticed because few cared and, if you were careful, you could sneak past those adults who did, whether they were your parents, your teachers, or the cops. It wasn't that hard. They were all too busy. The Mayor understood this. It had been the same for him. It took a long time to become something different. It helped if you met people who were different, or if you could get what is still called perspective. But it was hard.

The Mayor had begun to understand a lesson he had avoided learning ever since taking office. He could no longer be who he had once been, not promising scholarship student or visionary community organizer, not even idealistic councilman. He couldn't even get out of his vehicle to talk with kids who needed talking to, not anymore. He had to keep driving, or rather, riding, because he couldn't even drive himself.

That makes tonight's journey to the farm particularly exhilarating. The Mayor is back behind the wheel, doesn't need a map, knows exactly where he is going. And when he gets there, he will park the car and get out and talk to some people who still need talking to—they will hear him, he is certain, and so will the Folksinger. After all, he is, he believes, one of them. Still.

The Mayor worries that he'll be recognized, his cover blown.

He's famous, a household name, his victorious post-election face once smiling handsomely on the glossy covers of two—two!—national newsweeklies. At the chain-link gate to the farm, two young men tend a campfire contained in a squat metal half drum. One pokes at the embers with a long stick. The other lounges on a low-slung yard chair, a tin bucket in his lap, apparently shucking something he picks up from the ground. The unidentifiable product falls into the bucket with a ping. As the Mayor approaches, the young man tosses an object into the ashy cauldron and the flames sizzle and leap. A sharp odor rises. It makes the Mayor suddenly feel his accumulated sleeplessness, the chronic weariness that lurks in his joints, ready to let him stumble. The one with the stick points it silently to the hand-lettered sign leaning against the fence: NO WEAPONS, ALCOHOL, OR DRUGS. The tip of his stick glows. Back in his own days of sit-ins and protests, the Mayor and his young comrades scoffed at such measures. Later he accepted the rules and even enforced them like these two do, standing guard and playing peace cop. He draws a steadying breath. He allows himself to be patted down, lifting his sweat-shirted arms up and away from his sides.

"Nice shoes," says the one in the chair.

The Mayor thinks he's caught the other one swallowing a smirk, but he can't be sure. Like him, they have their fleece hoodies pulled up so that their hoods fall forward like the cowls of devout monks, shadowing their faces. One wears weathered leather work boots while the other is shod in rubber sandals that show his broad brown feet, toenails like thick shells. They wave him on, and so he goes, leaving them to stir their fire, shuck their mystery harvest into the tin bucket. His son's fancy shoes bounce him down the path, fine dust powdering the broad black toes.

The farm is crowded with bright domed tents pitched between plots, glowing with lantern light, sleeping bags, lying on the ground like fat wrinkled worms, rolled out between rows. The urgent whisperings of the still-awake rise. The night air is sharp, heavy with the industrious smell of growing crops, tilled soil, the prickly stench of pungent fertilizer. The plants seem to join the murmurs of the wakeful people: the corn stalks, the leaves and vines rustling with life. A line of poetry he memorized in college presents itself, unsolicited, full and whole despite the years that have lapsed since he buried it: "The force that through the green fuse drives the flower / Drives my green age." *The green fuse*, he thinks, *my green age*. He can't remember the poet's name, but he can feel his green force, even under the night sky. The city has vanished. The farm rises on all sides of him, lush, leafy green. The brown dirt path narrows.

The Mayor waits for someone to recognize him as he first bounces, then trudges along. Lanterns and strings of lights illuminate the path between the plots as if for a backyard party. All they see is his jeans, the oversized hoodie with its ghostly calaveras, the ridiculous shoes—a strange, harmless kid. He receives a few welcoming nods, half smiles already seeming to concede the defeat that awaits them in the morning. The young ones, their faces pinched in righteousness and weariness, assume he is just one of them, showing up for the inevitable showdown, with emergency phone numbers of the legal team written in ballpoint pen on his forearm.

Then, around a bend, a trio materializes, two men and a woman. They appear already ancient in their middle age, like the women and the men of his old neighborhood who'd observed him as he walked to school, as he carried groceries home from the store, as he hung out on the corner or in the park. When he was growing up, these strangers greeted him as if he were one of theirs—hijo, mijo—and whispered or called in passing, mostly in Spanish, sometimes in English: "Portate bien." "Be good." "Cuidate." "Stay out of trouble." They passed on wishes and warnings to him and the children like him with worried but hopeful eyes—smiling. The Mayor wondered what they had to smile about, these people who, like his mother, worked two and three jobs, jobs that took it all out of a person so at forty they seemed sixty, these people who never had a vacation, who seldom even slept in, who woke up tired and went to work anyway. Tonight these three look up and smile at him like he is the boy his clothes suggest he is. They pause with their tools in their hands—the two stout men with machetes, the woman with a shovel. At their feet, the plot of garden earth is turned as though for a grave. They harvest under the night sky, taking what they can, while they still can. Cactus paddles, corn, beans, hard green tomatoes like tiny fists. The waxy pale globes of the onions seem to glow, crushed stalks seeping pungent juice.

The Folksinger is, he knows, settled in comfortably in the famous black walnut tree somewhere in the center of the farm. All week the Mayor has been reading about the age and size of the goddamn black walnut tree. It is, apparently, extraordinary, over 120 feet tall. It is not merely a walnut tree but a California black walnut tree, a *Juglans californica*, to be mercilessly exact. The black walnut has, it seems, many medicinal qualities. It can cure maladies ranging from ringworm to psoriasis. Its oil is prized. To cut down the black walnut tree would be a crime, charge the hundreds of letters, emails, and calls his office has received and he, as the presiding mayor, would seem to be lumberjack-in-chief. To cut down the tree would bring a curse upon his head, threatened one letter, printed in all uppercase and signed CARYA. The young intern who delivered his mail informed him that Carya was the name of the Greek nut tree goddess.

"Sounds like a pretty minor goddess," the Mayor had joked.

"Not really," the intern, named Eva, had replied, her beautiful mouth unsmiling, "Her priestesses are those women who hold up the Acropolis on their heads."

"Ooh," he teased, "where did *you* go to school?"

"Same place as you," she said and turned to leave but then turned back, her long dark curls bouncing the way he liked, her thick dark eyebrows drawn low. Was she Greek? he wondered. He tried to recall her last name.

For what it was worth, Eva told him, she didn't want to see the tree cut down or the garden razed either.

"Is that all?" he had asked. He had stopped smiling too.

Now the walnut tree looms over him, taller than the telephone poles and as wide at its top as a house, spreading its branches as if it were posing for a centerfold in *Nut Meat Monthly*. Walnuts. Walnuts? He looks on the ground to see if any have fallen, but he doesn't really know what he's looking for. He imagines walnuts as he once saw them in the big open bins in the produce section at the grocery store, their knotty, woody shells like knuckles. When he was young, he'd play at the bin, plunging his hands deep and making the walnuts move in pleasing noisy waves. His mother never bought walnuts, never used the big pewter scoop to fill up a brown paper bag and weigh it on the swinging silver scale that hung from the ceiling. He never actually saw anyone buy them ever. And those were husked walnuts, processed for the market. City boy that he is, the Mayor has never seen one still on a tree.

A floodlight switches on from above and there she is, perched like a bright bird on a platform of two by fours and plywood, a treehouse raft hanging thirty feet above the ground, a canopy of blue hardware store tarpaulin strung above her. The Folksinger has spied him. Her eyes meet his with raptor-like certainty.

He'd half expected her to still be that barefoot girl-woman in the blue jeans, but tonight she wears the kind of clothing called "gear" in the slick adventure eco-tourism catalogs his wife leaves out on the coffee table, pages decorated with hopeful Post-it messages about adventures they could take if only he would tear himself away. A scarf, bright as a flag from a happy faraway country, is wrapped around her neck, and above that her proud head; her hair, now entirely silvery white, falls like a shawl woven from tinsel. She is smaller and older, a surprise. He does the math. As old, he realizes, as his mother would be. As old as she ever was, even when she hung on his bedroom wall. His mother's age, in fact.

"You missed the show," she says. Her legs swing free below the platform. Her feet are encased in boots that might climb mountains or leap over rocks at the riverside, laces as brilliant as ribbons. She pats her closed guitar case at her side.

"I'm mighty sorry about that," he says, flashing his trademark smile, "I've always wanted to hear you sing." This is true, but it oozes out like a bad pickup line. The "mighty" may have been too much. Sometimes he doesn't know when to stop. She is beautiful, elegant, strong. He is dressed as a teenage boy.

"I'm not hard to see," she replies. "I've come through this city every year for the last forty. Where were *you*?" She smiles but it's not the smile he wants. And her voice, the one he once had imagined as a heavenly river, is not giving him anything but dry rock bed.

The Mayor has worked it all out in his head, in the car. The Folksinger will recognize him. As indeed she has. Then he'll explain. He is good at that, explaining tough situations. There is only so much a mayor can do between the landlord and the law and he's done that and, *well*. She'll understand. The Folksinger is probably looking for a way out that dodges handcuffs and jail time. After all, she is no longer who she once was either—and he, the Mayor, the hero again, is there to provide her the graceful way out. He'll even give her a lift, perhaps back to the official residence where she can freshen up and spend what is left of the night in the fancy guest room. In the morning, they'll breakfast together. His wife might like that. This might score him some badly needed points at home too. He could make his famous huevos rancheros, squeeze fresh orange juice.

He reinvigorates his smile again, pulls down the hood to free his hair, and is about to launch into the plan when she speaks.

"You're not here to help," says the Folksinger. "You're not going to climb up this tree." Her legs keep swinging like she's a schoolgirl, not a sixty-something woman. Her boots bounce against each other. In her tone, there's the sound of a schoolyard taunt. "Are you?" she asks. "Are you?"

He has to look down now, away from her cascade of white hair and her swinging legs, her bright wise brown eyes that have seen it all: the firehoses in Birmingham, the dusty Central Valley picket lines, the bombs in Vietnam and in all the wars since then, hot and cold, at home and abroad, but when he does, all he sees are his son's stupid shoes poking out from under his blue jeans. Two hundred dollars of what the Folksinger would probably call sweatshop blood, shoes made in Vietnam by young women earning 25 cents an hour, bought by American kids who wouldn't bother to pick up a quarter on the ground. That war is long over but its grandchildren fight in another. Those easy equations still come to him quickly. Today's napalm is a sweatshop. He knows how she sees it. How she adds it all up. How she must now see him, once someone like her. He is about to say something that isn't exactly true or right, something he would never have said before he was elected: *Give up. Climb down from the walnut tree. Follow me. Please. Please.* He's about to work the moment—the pragmatic versus the ideal, the big picture. It's what he does now.

He hears their breath, their feet shuffling through the dust, the crunch of fallen leaves. They have an audience. The encampment gathers behind him. Young people. The three elders, with shovels and machetes. His private time with her is over now and what he might have done or said becomes even more impossible.

"You should really see what I can see," the Folksinger tells him. "From up here." Her voice has turned up a notch.

From up there, he thinks, she can see how his hairline has begun to recede like a slow tide, how it thins at the crown so that the scalp shines through. From up there, she can see what he can't say.

She pushes a pile of coiled rope over the edge of the platform and it unfurls like a question mark. A rope ladder. An invitation, a challenge, the nightmare of the Mayor's absent staff unable to advise, to caution, to feed him words that will make it all better. As had happened a week ago, when he was almost shouted down at a Skid Row press conference. Mid-speech, he was handed a card with ghostwritten retorts: *The protesters don't live here! Don't know what they are talking about!* But the Mayor knew, as did his staff, that those protesters had fed the hungry poor for decades. As a young community organizer, he'd sat at their hospitality soup kitchen table and eaten their nondenominational food. They had attended coalition meetings in church basements and college classrooms together, marched in picket lines, gone to jail. Anyone who had done the political work he had done in the city knew the people with the *Feed the Hungry* placards. But in that moment at the street-side podium, the Mayor denied them to the cameras.

Were his handlers here tonight, they would advise him to stay clear of the ladder and the beautiful woman at the other end. Hell, his staff would go nuts if they knew he was simply standing here, shuffling his feet in the dust. He reaches reflexively for his cell phone but, of course, his son's pouch pocket is empty. His cell phone is at home, in the inner pocket of his suit. The skulls on his sleeve grin.

The Mayor walks closer to the tree, and as he moves forward, he feels the crowd move with him. But he keeps his eyes on hers. He doesn't turn around.

"Mr. Mayor, I want to tell you a story," she says, leaning over the edge.

"Rapunzel?" he suggests, hoping for a laugh, a flirt of her eyes.

"No," she says. "True story, not a fairy tale. We are not children." She pushes her hair back with one hand.

The crowd titters.

"You know this one," she continues. "Once upon a time. Concord, Massachusetts. Ralph Waldo Emerson, famous American writer, visits his friend Henry David Thoreau, not-so-famous writer." She pauses. "Thoreau was locked up in the local jail. Do you know why?"

The Mayor answers without hesitation. "Thoreau refused to pay taxes that would have funded the Mexican-American War." He had learned that much in the university he and Eva had attended.

The crowd murmurs approval.

"See, I do know this story," the Mayor says.

"But it's been a while, hasn't it?" the Folksinger chides him affectionately, flashing a smile, luminous. She is speaking to him like his wife might, or his mother, an intimate, someone who knows what he has forgotten.

"Why do guys like that always have three names?" he asks. "Ralph Waldo Emerson. Henry David Thoreau." He doesn't like where this is going. He wants to play to the crowd, be the clown.

The Folksinger ignores him. Her voice grows louder as she addresses the people behind him. She leans forward, bracing herself on either side with hands that grasp the edge of the platform. "Now, the younger Thoreau often irritated his friend and patron. Emerson liked to think big thoughts, radical thoughts about nature and humanity. Transcendentalism. Thoreau agreed with Emerson but did more than just think. Thoreau took action, what we call today direct action. That made Emerson uncomfortable."

The crowd hisses at Ralph Waldo Emerson, with his three names and his Transcendentalism.

She continues, "So Emerson hears the news and goes down to the *hoosegow* to see his friend, to see what he can do. Perhaps he's thinking that Henry will hit him up for bail as Henry has, in the past, found Waldo's wealth easy to accept. When he sees his friend behind bars, Emerson asks, 'Henry, why are you in there?' His friend doesn't hesitate but famously answers: 'Waldo, the question is, why are you out there?'"

The Folksinger looks pleased with herself. Her cheeks pink up. There's even a little applause. She acknowledges it with a bow of her head, a sweeping embrace.

"I get it, *Henry*," the Mayor says.

The crowd laughs.

"Do you?" Her smile is wide now, but sad too.

There's a hush behind him.

"It's not that simple," he says. He looks behind himself for the first time, sees the dozens of people gathered, some wrapped in bedroll blankets or leaning on shovels, rakes. They're listening. Maybe he still has a chance to turn this his way. He turns back to the Folksinger, who is shaking her head ever so slightly. "It's not that simple," he repeats. "This farm, this garden, is not the Mexican-American War. It's not. It's . . ."

His smile falters into what he hopes passes for a sheepish grin. And the shiny words he had planned to use, his graceful way out, his poetry, stay where they are. In his head. Twirling like a mobile of what might have been. He should have known better. What he wants to ask her to do she cannot because she is sitting in that tree for others and he, the Mayor, is asking only for himself. He had known this and forgotten it somehow along the way. Nothing he can say will budge any of them, especially her.

When the Mayor reaches the gate and its lookout fire, burnt now to glowing coals, he thinks he hears the Folksinger beginning to sing. The two young sentries, still at their post, look up. They're both in chairs now, but their hands are busy, peeling, shucking, tossing. *Ping, ping, ping* into the bucket.

He feels their eyes on him, his uncovered head, the humiliation in his downward gaze. He nearly trips over something that rolls in his path. He kicks it out of the way, but it rolls back. He hears a snicker. The two guys at the fire again. He stoops to pick it up. A pod, palm-size, slightly oval, pale green. As he examines it, another rolls by. Then another. And another. They're playing with him. It could be worse, he thinks. They could be pelting him.

"Walnuts, man. They're everywhere," one calls out. The voice is surprisingly cheerful, warm.

"The tree," the other one says. "Take a piece with you before they take it down." His voice too is friendly. "Souvenir of the struggle."

The husk is firm, slightly furry, has a nice feel in his hand. The Mayor pockets it.

The Folksinger's voice soars. She sounds amplified but she's just taking advantage of what's left of the quiet night. Others join in, a chorus rises. It's a song he knows all the words to, an old hymn about being lost then found. She leads and the other voices follow and the garden with her singing becomes the church his young self imagined her voice created, one that Thoreau and his pal Emerson would have happily prayed in, knees in the dirt, hands digging, harvesting. The Mayor keeps his mouth shut. He doesn't look back.

His wife, he knows, must be waking up, stretching her arm across the white bed linens to feel for him, only to discover the pillow fresh, the tight sheet still tucked in on his side. She wears her long dark hair undone at night and he imagines how she pushes it out of her eyes and how her face tightens into worry. "Don't," he'd say if he could only get home in time but really, she *should* worry. His nights aren't always spent cruising the streets. Sometimes Javier takes him to an upscale apartment in the Valley where the Mayor doesn't have to knock, where his boyish gifts of Chinese takeout and supermarket flowers are received with exaggerated affection.

In the Camaro, he punches the radio on. Pre-set. His son's music blares, the urban hip-hop scene. He knows he should respect it, should be able to locate the healthy youthful rebellion in the music's rhythms and lyrics. He finds only his middle age, a sour mixture of impatience and intolerance. Though there is no one else to notice, he feels his shame spread. He hopes that the oldies station is still where it always was on the dial. He could use some good music to get him home, something familiar. But the oldies station with its soothingly predictable playlist of Top 40 is, of course, long gone. The Mayor considers his mistake even as he twists the dial. In place of Otis, Aretha, and Elvis, a shock jock rages, exhorting all-American blood donors to boycott blood donation because the Red Cross gives blood to all, including "illegals." The host declares that American blood should flow only in the veins of American citizens. This, he roars, is yet another example of America overrun by the alien swarm.

The Mayor switches off the radio, the Camaro backfires. He

jumps, as does the cool young blond woman in the car in the lane next to his. Her cell phone wraps around her ear, its mouthpiece extending like a stage microphone. She speaks intently into it. Her lips seem to form obscenities directed at him, his loud car, the space he takes up on the road. She glares, pulls forward, and cuts in front.

The Grand Biographer, he notices, has ditched him, bailed. The Mayor misses his commentary, the reassuring way he sees events, his big inspirational picture. It could be that he stayed back at the farm with the Folksinger. Maybe the Grand Biographer preferred her story to his. Who wouldn't? Maybe he is now writing another kind of story entirely.

For a while the Mayor just drives, like he used to. Surface streets. Finds a pleasing avenue, one with an encouraging green signal pattern and smooth flow of traffic and follows it until it hits the hills. Then he turns back, heads homeward. The sky is lightening, exposing the city. It's all strip malls and power lines, liquor stores and billboards, cinderblock walls layered with looping graffiti hieroglyphics. If the city at night is full of possibility, dawn is bleak, the bald light of the rising sun revealing all its limitations. The Mayor drives without sunglasses because he left in the middle of the night and hadn't foreseen this dawn. The morning sun shines directly in his tired eyes with its singular blinding glare.

He can't see a thing. He misses first one turn and then another. He circles around, trying to position the car in the correct lane, which requires a quick diagonal jump across the broken white lines, but the traffic is growing thick, slow. The morning commuters are not charitable to the driver in his hoodie in a '68 Camaro. Once more he fails. One driver leans on a horn. Another flips him off. He becomes stuck behind a bus that pauses for one signal change and then another as it labors to discharge passengers and load up new ones. The bus is not one of the sleek, clean-fuel fleet that he championed. It's ancient, large and lumbering, like the number 44 that kept him up at night in his mother's old apartment. Once, from the second-floor window, he watched his mother disembark, both hands weighted down with soft brown grocery sacks. This was before such bags had handles, before they were reinforced or cast in the plastic that kills marine mammals. She held one sack in each arm, balanced high on her hips. She waited for the traffic to pause so she could make her way across a street without a marked crosswalk. It was already dark, the end of a short winter day, and she was coming home from work. He had let himself in using the key she made him wear on a chain around his neck. His afternoon had been full of comic books and homework, rock 'n' roll played on the tinny radio that sat on the Formica kitchen table. He hoped that she would look up to see him, a good boy, framed in the kitchen window, and smile, but she didn't. She was too tired. Her arms were full. She kept watching the traffic, waiting for her turn. He had wanted to help her but he wanted more for her to see him there in the window. And so he stayed, poised, posed, smiling his good-boy smile until he realized that she was never going to look up, that she couldn't look up and keep going forward at the same time.

The squat back end of the bus shudders and exhales black diesel exhaust. He is blocked in. He can't do anything but wait and try again.

The Mayor thinks about his wife, his son, Javier, the security detail, his staff. His cell phone must be ringing and ringing then going to voicemail. So many people, he thinks, must be looking for him.

for Elena Popp

We Told You So

This morning the consequences of the new housing development became clear to commuters on the two-lane canyon road. A whopping 62 percent had voted for it, including Pam, who finally decided to turn off her car after seven minutes spent idling, watching her digital clock numbers collapse and re-form new numbers, larger ones, ever closer to the time she was supposed to be at the office. She'd never make it.

The local environmentalists had done what they usually do, railed against uncontrolled development and the beauty of the foothills and the fate of tiny animals with strange names, creatures that most people would probably kill if they ever found them on their properties, if they could even identify them. The arroyo toad. The black-tailed gnatcatcher. The orange-throated whiptail lizard. Some kind of snail. *A snail!* The eco-activists claimed that a vote for the development was a vote for twenty years of unabated construction. Now, this bright fall morning, Pam, whose four-year residency still marked her as a newcomer in the canyon, wondered if they were right. Pam didn't really care that much about the hills or their beauty or the tiny creatures that lived there. Her residence and the half acre it stood on had been a steal, an investment, and once she was done with her remodel, the house would look even more like a house should, more like those projected for Canyon View Estates. She could turn a tidy profit. She doubted that the development would impact the canyon at all. They couldn't even see the projected rolling carpet of red tile roofs from where they lived. But Pam did care about time, and, as a middle-aged woman, she knew how much she did and didn't have left. If her parents' simultaneous decline was a predictive measure, twenty years would about do it for her. Then she would be going the same way as that arroyo toad.

Then, as she adjusted her seat to a slight recline, she saw him. Her neighbor Angelo Vitalis, a retired teacher, standing on the side of the road just up ahead, where the asphalt gave way to dirt. Angelo had opposed the Canyon View Estates development and visited her house three times to ask her to change her mind. *Three times!* He was cheerful and good-natured despite his decades of teaching high school physics, or maybe because of it. He was handsome too, in a craggy Greek American way that the California sun somehow heightened and, Pam noticed, he was extremely fit from the vigorous biking he'd taken up in recent years and had pursued ever more seriously in the wake of his wife Margot's death. They had planned to travel the world on their bicycles. *Greece. A trip from the northern mountains all the way to the tip of the Peloponnese,* Margot had told her. But after she was killed, Angelo took to the local hills instead.

Pam found Angelo's visits, always with the proffer of a petition on a clipboard and a trifold informative brochure, highly offensive. She finally told him so. What right did he have to ask her how she intended to vote and then try to talk her out of it? He made her feel bad. She didn't like that.

This morning in the autumn sunshine illuminating the dry crisp hills like a floodlight, his mint-green racing bike tethered to a nearby utility pole, Angelo paced with his homemade sign greeting his neighbors: I TOLD YOU SO it read in the sturdy block letters of a lifelong high school classroom teacher. When he saw Pam in her reliably shiny Lexus in the stalled lineup, he waved and winked. He wore black Lycra bike shorts, his brilliant orange jersey unzipped. A small festival of his white chest hair caught the morning light.

Pam felt her heart jump a bit and, without thinking, she waved back, her fingers flapping up and down to touch her palm. Then she smiled. She couldn't help it.

Angelo smiled back and flashed her a thumb's-up. Now she was mad at him for that too. He probably thought he had changed her mind.

In her rearview mirror, Pam spied a tiny car crawling up on the right in the bike lane. *The bike lane!* The driver of the tiny sports car was trying to sneak past everyone instead of waiting their turn. Pam leaned on her horn to object. She was no rebel, but she was a rule follower. You wait your turn like everybody else. You stay in your lane.

Angelo's smile grew. He nodded, enthusiastically pointing to Barefoot Roy, one of the canyon's cartoony elders, those men sporting long white beards like the silver miners who gave the canyon its name. Barefoot Roy stood next to him, beard tumbling, feet bare, of course, as they always had been, so the story goes, ever since he returned from Vietnam. He held another obviously Angelo-lettered sign that read HONK TO SAVE OUR CANYON. Pam's honk had unintentionally started something. Other cars joined in and formed a bleating chorus. The tiny sports car stopped its sneaky creep in the bike lane. Angelo beamed.

❦

The white line separating the car lane from the designated bike lane was slightly raised and six inches wide per State of California regulations. Angelo had learned this during the trial of the man who struck and killed Margot nearly two years earlier. It happened on a Friday morning. Spring. Angelo was teaching AP physics. His final semester before his much-anticipated retirement after decades of teaching.

Margot had been traveling on her Bianchi Via Nirone 105 in the designated bike lane that stretched along the twelve scenic miles of canyon road but that, on approach to the toll road, abruptly vanished as a right-hand turn lane took its place. While Margot steadily pedaled forward, navigating this shift, the eighty-five-year-old driver of a silver minivan suddenly realized that he needed to turn right so he wouldn't miss his opportunity to merge onto the toll road. The driver had been at the reservoir that morning to take photos. A bald eagle had been sighted there, hanging out like he owned the place. These were his hobbies: birds and photos. Now he was returning home to Yorba Linda on the other side of the hills, in the flatlands.

Although the defendant was never called to the stand, the motorcycle cop first on the scene testified that the driver had told him that he had seen Margot earlier and believed her to be behind him, not to the side, nor, as it turned out, ahead of him. His estimated speed was thirty-five to forty miles per hour, below the posted legal limit. The photos show she hit the middle of the broad windshield and then flew several yards, her cherished bicycle crumpling under the van. Margot was wearing a helmet, of course, but died of severe head injuries the next day. She never woke up. The driver, elderly but unimpaired, with an impressively clean sixty-year record, was charged with misdemeanor vehicular manslaughter which, if he were convicted, would have resulted in suspension of his license and a fine.

The trial lasted less than a week. Police, eyewitnesses,

paramedics, doctors, the defendant's ophthalmologist, the owner of the bicycle shop where Margot purchased her gear and participated in safety classes all testified. Deliberations lasted for three days. On the last day, the Santa Anas started up and before the mid-morning break, two wildfires, one in Laguna and the other in the canyon, blazed. Angelo, in his one good suit, the same one he wore at commencement each year, monitored the fires from the court building's cafeteria windows. It didn't look good. When he'd arrived to buy the cardboard cup of black coffee he would nurse all morning, the twin peaks of the Saddleback were clear. Now the summits of Santiago and Modjeska had begun vanishing behind rapidly billowing clouds of black smoke. His coffee, no *ellinikós kafés,* to be sure, but bitter and dark enough for his mood, had grown cold. There was no one at home he could call to see how bad the fires were in the neighborhood. Then he had the thought that terrified and later shamed him: *Let it burn*. What did he really have to lose?

At that moment, the prosecutor came looking for him. "Call me Sanaz," she had said that first day when they met in her office. Sanaz Motamedi had explained that this was a long-shot case but one worth pursuing. Now it was ending. Angelo stood, abandoning his coffee cup on the table where he had a window seat to the spreading fires.

That morning, in his suit pocket, he had found the folded commencement program from that final graduation. He fumbled for it. The senior class had seen fit to include a mention of his recent loss. He offered the program to Motamedi. He couldn't call her Sanaz, he just couldn't. He was too old and she was, well, a *prosecutor*. "Look," he said and then put it in her hands.

Sanaz Motamedi was still young, a recent stand-out graduate from the local public university's law school, snapped up by the DA's office—which, she confessed to him in an unguarded moment, she knew needed attorneys like her to fulfill their diversity initiative. "Orange County," Angelo remarked knowingly.

She examined the program with respect, but Angelo suddenly felt embarrassed. Why had he handed it to her? Why had he kept it in his pocket in the first place? Ever since Margot's death, Angelo, once as disciplined and logical as the equations he drilled his students on, had grown prone to increasingly impulsive acts and thoughts like this one, like his sudden wish for his house to burn.

"What thoughtful kids," Sanaz remarked with pro forma appreciation as she returned the booklet to him. She knew he and Margot hadn't had children of their own. "But we should go now," she added, smooth, firm, moving him along, doing her job.

The jury had deadlocked, just like that, as if they too wanted to get home in time to evacuate. A mistrial. Sanaz met with the few jurors who lingered afterward, including the three disappointed ones who had voted to convict. She informed Angelo that it was unlikely her office would again press charges. "I don't think," she told him, "we'd prevail if we did." She alluded to the everyday prejudice against cyclists, even law-abiding ones such as his wife. One juror had told her that another juror remarked after deliberations that he thought cyclists like Margot were just asking for it, riding their bikes everywhere. Others had nodded.

"Besides," the prosecutor said, "I doubt he'll ever drive again. That's what you really want, right?" She was speaking of the octogenarian bird-watching defendant from Yorba Linda, who had been accompanied to court every day by his two daughters. One of the daughters drove. Angelo saw them arrive together in the parking lot. In the year between the accident and the trial, the driver had withered further into old age, resembling, Angelo thought, a heron: tall and stooped, deliberate, wary.

What Angelo really wanted, of course, was Margot and that

late life they had planned together, still so much of it ahead. Years. At least fifteen, maybe twenty, if they were lucky. Once they had felt lucky. What did he really want now? Yes, that particular old, dangerous driver off the road was a good start. Angelo hadn't wished for jail time or punishment, only accountability, acknowledgment of responsibility. Something. The old man had never spoken to Angelo, no doubt following the advice of his attorney. Angelo shook Sanaz's hand. Thanked her. Accepted the regretful gazes of those lingering jurors and courtroom officials. Patted the folded commencement program in his pocket. Good kids.

He drove back into the smoke, eyes smarting, right past, as he had to every day, the site where the minivan collided with Margo's bicycle. Two moving objects in space. Acceleration. Velocity. Displacement. The intersection where the two objects met. The white lines on the blacktop approximating the ones he used to draw on the blackboard of the high school a few miles down that same road.

Within a week of Margot's death, a local advocacy group had installed a "ghost bike" nearby, chained to the fence a few yards away. Angelo didn't initially know who they were. One day, the bike, painted a spectral stark white, just appeared, adorned with his wife's name and plastic flowers, a roadside shrine. When the first memorial disappeared a few weeks later, it was replaced in short order. A story in the newspaper identified the organizers as a loose-knit group of do-gooder cyclists. Sometimes, as today, Angelo stopped at Margot's ghost bike, pulling over, off the road and onto the shoulder, getting out of his car to stretch his legs.

This was the spot where Margot used to say the city ended and the canyon began, a big swoop of wild. When it was clear, you could see all the way to the Pacific and even Santa Catalina Island, stretched out as if sleeping on the horizon. Not so beautiful today. Wind-whipped trash was trapped, flapping against the fence. The dry brush on the hills looked ready to combust. The air was orange, thick. The ghost bike had been buffeted by the winds but was still standing, its bouquet of artificial flowers left by strangers intact. There was absolutely nothing for Angelo to do here. Clearly, what he needed to do was go home, secure the house, see if anyone else needed help. In times like these, Judy the widow next door required someone to catch her nervous cat and put it in the pet carrier and corral Fergus, her tiny yapping dog. Sue, who ran the chicken co-op, might need help rounding up the birds. There was always something to do in the neighborhood, someone to do it for. Angelo still felt lucky, he realized, driving deeper into the smoke. He was still here. There was still something to save.

The one-year anniversary of what they now called the Wildcat Canyon Fire was also, for Angelo, the anniversary of the deadlocked jury. But now it also had become the birthday of the Save the Canyon League, first delivered into public view on that October morning when he and Barefoot Roy took to the road. The SCL met monthly in the library's community room to strategize and paint their signs.

The local library was also where Angelo had, under the guidance of Rich, a research librarian who shared his passion for cycling and justice, discovered the history of the Bicycle Safety Task Force. The lifespan of task forces is short. They complete their task and then disband. This BSTF completed its task over ten years earlier, delivering a report to the County Board of Supervisors that clearly identified six ranked places that merited safety improvements, with Margot's murderous intersection listed as number one. "Northbound cyclists wishing to continue traveling along the canyon road must move left as traffic accelerates onto the toll road," the report stated. The task force recommended that the county add signage prompting drivers to "yield to bikes" as well as designated green bike lanes. That was never done, of course. The board argued that the state department of transportation, Caltrans, was responsible for that particular intersection. Caltrans argued that the county was. And nothing was done for ten years.

Pam had her nails done that week, a reward for suffering through the longer, slower morning commute. While her fingernails were kept to a sober corporate clear suitable for her position, her toenails now sported palm trees and shorelines, breaking blue waves topped with white crests, each one a tiny advertisement for a tropical adventure that even she knew could not possibly exist. But on the weekend, when time was her own, she liked seeing her toes in her sandals, each nail sporting a slice of beach. One day, she promised herself, she'd get there and maybe stay there. Some kind of timeshare. Cabo or Costa Rica. After she'd sold this place, paid off her parents' debts. Until then, her toenails offered a glimpse.

This Saturday afternoon, Pam settled on her porch in the sun, sitting in one of her two red Adirondack chairs, reading the new glossy home magazine that had arrived in the mail. October was still like summer in Southern California. The magazine declared that fall was one of the most revered seasons of the year and the perfect time to refresh your house's porch. Her porch could use some refreshing. She was sipping a rum drink she had mixed just for this occasion, with more waiting in a festive pitcher, when she saw Angelo returning from his bike ride. She expected him to keep pedaling past but instead he turned into her dirt driveway.

"I'll keep my distance," he called out as he stopped and straddled his bike a few yards away. "Too stinky!" he said by way of explanation, waving away sweat with self-mocking gestures. Once again he was encased in glistening body-hugging Lycra, tiny black fingerless gloves. When he snapped off his helmet, she saw that his hair had begun to grow out, in thin silver curls that grazed his shoulders.

"Yes?" she said, as coolly as possible. What could he want? He had no clipboard. He was dripping sweat and despite his distance she could smell his funk. She saw him glance at her feet, her tropical toes. Could he see the palm trees?

"I've been thinking," he said. "I know you're a lawyer, but what kind of law do you do?"

No, she thought, he can't possibly imagine she would represent his group against the development. She sold real estate on the side. She was becoming what some of her friends called a "house flipper." It was as she feared. Angelo must have taken her morning honk for a change of heart.

"Not the kind you want," she said, sipping from her tall, chilled glass. Pam handled estates mostly. She once had bigger ambitions but settled for estate planning. The work was steady.

"No, no, no," he said. "You misunderstand. This is about Margot."

Pam had liked Margot. At least in theory. Margot had been the first neighbor on the street to welcome her, bringing a basket of goodies: local eggs along with a pitch to join Sue's chicken coop co-op; a flashlight and candles for power outages; cards for various services (tree trimming, bee removal, septic tank) and a canyon bumper sticker, *Keepin' it Rural.* Pam declined the offer to join the co-op but accepted Margot's extra egg bounty every time it was offered, which turned out to be fairly often. In return Pam would pour another glass of whatever she might be drinking and

Margot would linger. They became porch pals. Pam's porch had a sweeping view of the sycamores that grew alongside the creek bed and turned a brilliant green in the spring and gold in the fall. They didn't talk much but they talked easily. A little canyon gossip went far. Pam was genuinely sad when Margot was killed, attended the memorial held at the community room at the library, posted condolences on the NextDoor Neighbor chat board.

"What are you drinking?" Angelo asked.

"Dark 'n' Stormy," Pam replied. She was proud of her mixology skills. A couple years earlier, some of the girls at work had signed up for a series of classes with a bartender and learned how to mix their favorite cocktails. Pam was a natural, it seemed. Hers had flair. For a while she had had the bartender too, until that, like all her other romances, had fizzled out.

Angelo seemed to be waiting for more explanation.

"Ginger beer, rum, and lime," she said. "A little simple syrup. Crushed ice."

"Margot liked rum." Angelo stood there. Even though the afternoon sun was still shining and he had been sweating mere moments earlier, he began to shiver. His skin, Pam could see, was developing goose pimples.

"Are you okay?" she asked, beginning to rise.

"I think I just need to sit. Can I sit?" His voice was thin. He leaned his bike against the tree, hung his helmet by its strap on the handlebars.

"Sit, sit." Pam was up and out of her chair and offering its twin to Angelo, who was, she reminded herself, despite his other annoying behaviors, older and a widower and a neighbor. Margot's husband. Deserving of a chair. Margot's chair. "Something to drink?"

"I have water on my bike." He pointed. His color wasn't good.

"I'll go get you some fresh."

By the time she returned, Angelo already seemed better. He drank the glass of water she gave him and then accepted two fingers of the Dark 'n' Stormy.

"Not bad," he remarked. "And I don't even like rum."

"The ginger beer makes it," she said, "plus the dark rum. You have to have good dark rum. Goslings Black Seal is the best. None of that Captain Morgan or Bacardi crap."

"No," he said agreeably, "none of that crap." He smacked his lips on "crap."

"Are you making fun of me?" Pam might have been a little drunk. Rum in the sun. When she got drunk, she got sensitive and when she got sensitive, she began to suspect the worst in everyone. This could make her belligerent. That's the word Rico the bartender boyfriend had used. Belligerent. He said it made her ugly. Pam wondered what was happening now. How had her pushy neighbor ended up on her porch, drinking her good rum?

"No, not all. I am admiring your standards. Life is too short for crappy rum." Angelo drained his glass.

"May I?" he asked, pointing to the pitcher. Without waiting for Pam to answer, he poured himself another short one. "What do you know about suing the county?" he asked, blue eyes beneath his wild gray brows suddenly alert. "What do you know about suing the state?"

His many years in the classroom had taught Angelo how to appraise people, judge what they were capable of, take stock of their potential even if they were, like most teenagers, oblivious of their own considerable abilities, uninterested in or even frightened of learning more than they already knew. It was Newton's first law: "Every body continues in its state of rest, or uniform motion in a straight line unless compelled to change that state by forces impressed upon it." Angelo the teacher was that impressive force on generations of suburban teens who would prefer to remain resting or continue as they always had. And Pam was like one of those students who showed up to class out of duty, flush with hormonal resentment. Student Pam would have done the homework because she wasn't a bad student, but she wasn't going to raise her hand. She was just going to take the test and then get the hell out of there.

Angelo had seized the rum-drunk porch moment, swiftly scrambling to his house, returning with his files, the task force report, the history of accidents at the same location and his own documents about Margot's case. He watched now as Pam spread the contents of the manila file folders out on her dining room table as if laying it for a fancy dinner.

Pam had lost her crouched defensive stance that Angelo knew so well from his door-to-door canvassing days. When she contemplated something that truly interested her, whether it was her home improvement magazines or the papers she was now sorting, she became a different creature. Here she was, padding around barefoot on her gleaming wooden floors, almost dancing, whistling under her breath as she scanned the documents. Her countenance was attentive, not dismissive, and when she looked at him, her eyes smiled along with her mouth. Her brown hair, professionally streaked with blond highlights and usually pinned up and back, was hanging loose.

Pam insisted that Angelo sit at the head of the table, so he did, presiding over its butcher block, sipping his topped-up Dark 'n' Stormy poured from the pitcher Pam had refreshed in his absence. It was the weekend after all. He was retired. He'd be walking home, not driving. She slid a bowl of peanuts toward him. Spanish, salty, slipping out of their dark papery skins. "Eat something."

It was almost nice to have someone tell him what to do. Sit here. Drink this. Eat that.

Pam squinted at the map attached to the final report, drawing her finger along the highway, comparing it to the accident scene photo fanned out across the tabletop. "This is gold," she announced.

"Gold?" Angelo winced. But Pam didn't seem to notice his grimace. She had become an eager and ruthless attorney instead of a slightly inebriated woman on a porch or a defensive neighbor fending off a petition.

"Pure gold," she confirmed. "Even I could win this."

The accident scene photos didn't include Margot, though her presence could be discerned by evidence flags, spray paint, skid marks, vehicle debris, shattered glass, and what was poetically referred to as the "final resting place." The newspaper clippings featured her last official school district photo, smiling, her dark hair cut in a short, blunt bob and bangs as it had always been. Margot, a film studies minor, remained French New Wave long after the wave had crashed. Mrs. V, she was called, a popular teacher at the canyon's rural elementary school, known for her ability to smuggle *français* into almost every lesson. When the school had closed a few years back due to low enrollment, the financial crash, and the casual disregard so often directed at canyon residents, Margot opted for early retirement rather than transfer to another school. That's when she took up cycling, leaving every morning when Angelo did, cruising the stretch of two-lane highway she liked to call her *Tour de Canyon*.

It was Margot who told him about Pam's "situation," as she put it. The only child of parents who developed different but challenging health conditions that required assistance beyond that covered by their health plans. As a result, Pam had spent the previous ten years helping her parents die. "That's why she is the way she is," Margot said by way of explanation. "Hard. Bitter. Closed. I feel sorry for her."

Angelo recalled Margot's assessment as he watched Pam rifle through the papers. He was no lawyer, but it seemed to Angelo he had a case. That's what Rich the librarian claimed. And when Motamedi had followed up with him, she indicated the same. "If you ask me," Sanaz admitted, "the Board of Supervisors gets away with murder because no one stands up to them." Even though her cell phone connection was breaking up, Angelo could hear the righteousness in her voice, which was what he liked first and best about her. "I shouldn't say that," she said. "I can't advise you on your course of civil action. You know my office can't be involved." Angelo understood. The young prosecutor was like an ambitious AP student who knows more than she can possibly use on the big test.

Pam left the table and returned with a yellow legal pad, a pen, and one of those pre-packaged snack platters of sliced cheese and salami. "Open that, would you?" she said, pushing the plastic tray toward him as she settled into a chair. The squares of cheddar, salami rounds, and cornichons glistened.

"If you're going to do this, we need to start now," Pam said, all business. "In California you have two years starting from the date of the underlying incident to file toward seeking a legal remedy for the death of an individual caused by the wrongful act or neglect of another."

"Sounds like I picked the right attorney," Angelo remarked. He knew that salami shouldn't be paired with rum, but the thin round sure tasted good, especially when rolled together with a cheese slice. Sharp, spicy, agreeably chewy. Epicurean Margot would have objected, but then again, Margot would have also forbidden Angelo to partake of any of the shiny, high-sodium finger foods before him. She was determined he would live forever, or nearly so.

"You did, but any lawyer could win this," Pam said. "Why me?"

On the top of the legal pad he saw she had written *Margot Vitalis* and *DOD April 8* in blue ink. Her handwriting was bold and clear. Pam had spelled Margot's name correctly. She remembered the day of her death.

"That's why," Angelo said, tapping the paper with his index finger, greasy with salami oil. It left a shiny smudge. "Margot liked you. You remember who she was."

Pam's attentive face blurred a bit as if he had smeared it with his oily finger. But it was just those tears that still watered his eyes in unexpected moments. His voice was gravelly. "Why *not* you?"

Roger Campbell, the county supervisor who represented the canyons and foothills even though he himself lived in the suburbs, always wore a Western shirt and blue jeans when he appeared at community meetings at the library. Sometimes he even rode up on his Harley instead of cocooned within his Tesla, joking about stopping off at the local biker bar on the way home. Angelo, like many, never bought Campbell's shtick. Barefoot Roy saw through him too.

"Here comes the Kmart cowboy," Roy would announce loud enough for everyone to hear when the supervisor showed up post-wildfire or flood or mudslide to explain just what the county would do. Not much, as it turned out. And what they wouldn't do, which was a lot. Supervisor Campbell sounded like that biased juror who blamed Margot for her own death. Canyon residents were just asking for it. What did they expect? It seems their elected official thought they were just like those arroyo toads.

So when Angelo finally saw the supervisor in his own natural habitat, the bimonthly Board of Supervisors meeting in the Hall of Administration in downtown Santa Ana, he was not surprised. Suit and tie, tiny enamel American flag pin on his lapel, classic wingtip Oxfords, red tie.

Barring any unforeseen circumstances, the supervisor would announce a settlement, Pam assured him. For months their item had lingered on the agenda in the closed session along with other claims characterized as "significant exposure to litigation." But when Caltrans settled last month, an impressive six figures, pressure grew. Today was the day. Pam was confident. Her open toe slingbacks highlighted the return of tropical motifs to her toes. She had already booked a celebratory trip to Maui.

For the proceedings, Angelo donned his one good suit and parked where he had for the trial. As was his habit, he drove all the way to the top of the parking structure. Today the top level afforded an especially spectacular view as the previous day's rainstorm had scoured the sky.

Barefoot Roy, who accompanied him, approved. "Look at that," he said, his arms spread wide. Snow frosted the distant San Gabriels. Roy had dressed up for the occasion in chinos pressed by his wife Maureen and a dark-blue plaid Pendleton for the post-storm chill, his equivalent of a suit and tie. His feet, true to his name, remained bare. He noticed Angelo's gaze drop down and quickly assured him that his lack of shoes wasn't going to be an issue. "First I claim a sincere religious belief," he said, "then I show them this." He held up his good conduct medal worn around his next on a thick chain.

"Efficiency. Honor. Fidelity," Angelo read aloud. The medal was a warm, worn bronze, eagle on one side, wreathed star on the other.

"Gets them every time," Roy said. "Plus it's good for getting out of jury duty. I already done my duty."

They were early so Roy allowed Angelo to point out landmarks. The old county courthouse, stalwart, red brick, over a hundred years old, where, as it happened, both men had married their brides. The newer courthouse, where Angelo had attended what he still thought of as Margot's trial and where Barefoot Roy routinely evaded his civic duty. The Office of Vital Records, where Angelo had stood in line to get a copy of Margot's death certificate and, if he had so desired, could have requested his birth record as well. It was all here. The Civic Center. The county seat.

Barefoot Roy turned out to be right. They were let in without any trouble. Pam was waiting for them. Angelo saw her take in Roy's feet, his thick calloused soles, the broad talon-like nails. She grinned. She seemed in better spirits these days.

"Let's sit up front," she said.

The meeting made its way through an ecumenical invocation and the pledge, with Pam pulling both men to their feet with a stern look. Angelo thought he saw Campbell's eyes snag on them, an unlikely front-row trio: Roy with his wispy miner's beard, Angelo in his suit and now sporting a ponytail, Pam in her bright silvery courtroom suit.

"After they read the resolutions, they'll announce the decisions taken in closed session," Pam whispered. "That's us."

Angelo saw Motamedi enter the hall. She too had let her hair grow long. She sat where they could see each other. She winked.

Pam was right. After the resolutions honoring various civic-minded citizens and community initiatives along with the required posing with the declarations and smiling photo ops, the clerk read out the decisions. As predicted, the supervisors had matched Caltrans dollar for dollar. It was as anti-climactic as listening to the Emergency Broadcast System sound its test tone until Campbell interrupted the clerk and asked for a point of personal privilege.

Barefoot Roy grunted and said something, which only Angelo and Pam could hear, about where Campbell could stuff his "pointy privilege." Campbell had a microphone so everyone could hear him. The supervisor, apparently the only dissenting vote on the settlement, read from remarks he'd obviously prepared for the occasion, an occasion that, he pointed out, was happening more and more frequently as citizens who could not take responsibility for their own misfortune and poor decisions instead blamed the government and came begging for compensation, stealing taxpayer money that could and should be spent in better ways. As he'd been allotted ten minutes, Campbell said much more but Angelo didn't hear it. He was out of there. He couldn't bear to listen to Margot's name in Campbell's mouth, to hear once again that her death was her own fault. He left, the security guard opening the door for him as if on cue.

The bench he found was in the sun, a block of cement resembling a giant eraser. The Civic Center had always been a massive island of concrete with serviceable buildings that didn't soar so much as squatted in the middle of Santa Ana. Its recent renovation added more concrete, though there seemed to have been a good-faith attempt to landscape with low-maintenance native trees and drought-tolerant plants. Angelo noted the efforts: paloverde trees, some kind of live oak, and planters filled with sage and succulents. The plants themselves seemed to be withholding their commitment to thrive. But there was still time. Angelo could see a future where these fast-growing trees offered cooling shade and hummingbirds returned to investigate the flowering buds. But at the moment it was still all theoretical. Some disease could sweep through, or the board could vote to reinstate jacaranda and bougainvillea, a return to palms and eucalyptus. Anything could happen.

Soon his friends found him. They were his friends, weren't they? Barefoot Roy, of course, his fellow troublemaker. But even Pam, who now, more often than not, motioned him to join her on her porch as he returned from his weekend rides in the hills. And prosecutor Motamedi, who called from time to time just to see how he was doing. These women had somehow become his friends too.

Roy sat down beside him while the two women stood nearby. Motamedi was immediately reassuring. "You know that was just Campbell blowing off steam, right? He's just one vote. Can't change a thing."

"Hot air," Roy agreed. "Sour grapes too."

They spoke louder than they needed to. The plaza was deserted. Everyone else was still inside.

"Yes," Angelo said, nodding. "All that. Hot, steamy, sour grapes."

"I think I voted for him," Pam said. "Twice." She shuddered.

"A lot of people did," Angelo said. "He looks good on a billboard, on a shiny mailer. He says all the right stuff." He consoled her with surprising ease. "But you won't make that same mistake again. Now you know." He didn't add that Campbell would soon be termed out. Pam would never be offered the chance to make that same mistake. Not that it meant Campbell was done. The Board of Supes was just a launching pad. He was eyeing Sacramento, perhaps even Washington. Now it was Angelo's turn to shudder.

"We should be celebrating," Roy pointed out. "We won."

"We did indeed," observed Angelo. There they were, sitting with their victory in the Civic Center plaza. Not that anyone looking at them, had there been anyone looking, could see the million-plus. The two settlements would fund the Save the Canyon League for real. Paid organizers. A consulting attorney. Money enough to purchase green space outright. And the county and Caltrans would finally do what they should have done years earlier: address the dangers to cyclists at that intersection of the canyon road—orange signs, a high-profile designated bike lane, thick stripes on the asphalt, adjusted speed limits. Margot's intersection!

"This is what this kind of victory feels like," Motamedi observed. Her smile turned down at the edges. "You wish you didn't have to fight so hard to win, so when you do, even when you do . . ." Her voice trailed off. Her beautiful young hand made a motion in the air that resembled a Mobius strip.

Angelo had told himself he wasn't going to cry, and he didn't. If any of them had said her name, he would have. Instead, he stood up as if, in the standing, the tears brimming in his eyes could be reabsorbed back into his body. And so they were. "I think we're done here," he said. "Thank you."

"We did good," Barefoot Roy added.

"We did," Angelo agreed. "Good enough."

False Flag

When her next-door neighbor Matthew finally peeled the enormous red, white, and blue "Q" decal from the back window of his white pickup after his presidential candidate's defeat, Linda imagined that he, unlike the candidate, was conceding. Matthew even removed the vintage "Lock Her Up" sticker from the bumper along with the even older "Nope." His Chevy was now as blank as a Styrofoam cup. He lowered the candidate's flag on his driveway flagpole, replacing it with the American flag Linda had first seen flying there when she arrived in the rural Southern California canyon years earlier: like Matthew, divorced, unlike him, not childless. The months-old beard that grizzled Matthew's face along with the out-of-character ponytail snaking down his back she chocked up to late-stage pandemic grooming. Soon, she hoped, Matthew would return to his old self, a gruff but reliable neighbor who shaved and was dependable in a crisis, whether it was a jump-start, fallen tree, or wildfire evacuation.

Then Linda noticed that Matthew's recent absence coincided with the January 6 unrest.

Her daughter Willow was baking that day, an elaborate Rosca de Reyes, the Mexican Kings' Day cake shaped like a crown, rolled, and filled with dried fruit. The girl had risen at dawn to chop nuts and raisins, and then to candy orange peel, her long black hair, streaked with hot pink, pulled back in a bright braid. The pandemic had inspired Willow to dye her hair and bake a cake each week, activities Linda encouraged. Keep them busy, her mother, a single parent of five girls, used to say. It was the one parenting tip Linda had taken from her childhood.

The rosca was a yeasted cake, requiring two rises. It kept the teenager busy that day creating the cake while she and Linda watched the livestream from the nation's capital together. What had begun as an ordinary Wednesday at home, asynchronous school for Willow and work duties and puttering around the house for Linda, became something else entirely mid-morning when Willow's AP government teacher Mr. Sawaya sent the entire class an emergency extra credit text: "Tune into PBS now and write what you see. 100 points EC." Hours later, as Wednesday, January 6 became Thursday, January 7, Willow was still writing. Finally, in the wee hours, the vice president declared Joseph Robinette Biden Jr. of Delaware the forty-sixth president of the United States.

Willow sat curled up on the couch, wrapped in blankets, laptop balanced on her lap, tapping away, one long hank of her hair hanging from her mouth. This was a new habit, born of the pandemic, this hair twirling and sucking. Linda let it be.

Willow's rosca had risen nicely, becoming golden in the oven, its crown of candied orange slices, cherries, and figs gleaming beneath its sugary glaze. The cake had sustained them during the Capitol's siege and evacuation, and the midnight return of the electors. Linda was grateful for the thoughtful news anchors who could answer her daughter's questions better than she could. No parent wants to give their child "I don't know" as an answer to anything.

The uneaten half of the crumbly sweet crown would be more than enough for breakfast. Perhaps one of them would find the plastic stand-in for Baby Jesus still hidden inside. Willow had tucked one of her tiny Totoro figurines, a cheerful forest creature, deep into the dough.

On TV, weary reporters were signing off against a montage of photos and video feed of the day: the unstoppable stream of marchers, bodies swollen by tactical gear, their flags and signs turned into weapons, their weapons trained on Capitol police, their chants, their rage, the makeshift gallows with its orange noose, the assault on that iconic white domed building.

"Who are these people, Mom?" Willow asked, closing her computer. "Where did they come from?" It was 1:00 A.M., the room lit now only by the TV and its seemingly endless replay of the day's remarkable events. Willow expertly wound the long slick strand of hair around her index finger, pink-black, pink-black, like a kind of striped candy Linda vaguely remembered from childhood. *What was it called? Good and Plenty?*

Linda sighed. It was just the two of them, as it had been for some years now. She had to field all the questions, respond to all the demands. She often felt that ache of the single parent. She wondered about her own mother, the tough questions that she and her sisters may have asked her—not that Linda, her youngest, recalled asking her much of anything, so afraid was she of getting on her mother's bad side. Five girls was just too much. Still, she remembered when Robert Kennedy was shot across town. Linda was too young to stay up late enough to watch the story unfold on television, but her mother and her oldest sister Carol had. Her mother wasn't what you would call political, but she had liked the Kennedys, handsome Catholic family men. *Maybe you'll marry a Kennedy*, she teased her daughters. *There's enough of them, there's enough of you.* Two of Carol's friends had worked on the campaign and were at the ballroom that night. Carol hoped to see her pals on TV wearing their jaunty white straw boater hats, the ones adorned with the red, white, and blue bands, images of the candidate and the slogan "KENNEDY WILL WIN!" She didn't. When Linda and her sisters left for school that morning the senator was still alive, but the next day he was dead. Unlike her own daughter, Linda never asked why. Of course, it was only a single shooter, at the end of a decade of too many crazed lone gunmen, the second high-profile assassination within two months. January 6, whatever it was, felt different, looked different. So many raging thousands, not just one.

"Good questions, Will," Linda replied. "We'll see what the news says tomorrow. But now it's late." Her daughter nodded. That was enough of an answer for now. Meanwhile, Linda was already wondering if she knew the identity of at least one.

Matthew had asked Willow to feed his chickens while he was gone. Willow was the one Matthew had relied upon for years now whenever a trip—Vegas, a 49ers game, a fishing excursion, some family gathering— took him away. It was a neighborly duty the girl especially enjoyed as it allowed her to unlock the big gate that separated their backyards and swing it wide open, freeing his eager flock to roam and forage in their wild untended garden. Once upon a time, canyon lore goes, their two lots had been owned by brothers who built identical modest houses for their identical modest lives: two stories, two bedrooms, big front porches, a bit of mid-century midwestern in the Southern California foothills. His chickens in their yard seemed part of that shared past.

Matthew returned in the late afternoon on Thursday, pulling into his driveway at his usual high speed, sending gravel spraying and inspiring a chorus of complaints from the squirrels who fled to the surrounding oak trees. Linda waved from the porch where she sat with that morning's newspaper. She waved because, well, that's what you did in the canyons. You waved. To everybody. She was still looking for a good answer to her daughter's late-night questions: *Who were these people? Where did they come from?* The newspaper had some answers.

The Matthew who emerged from the truck was clean shaven, cheeks shiny, eyes bright. His old-school crew cut was back. He hauled his duffel out of the back and responded to Linda's greeting by lifting his now-bare chin in her direction. On the truck's broad dashboard, Linda glimpsed the distinctive parking receipt— a cardboard cowboy hat—from the local airport, named for the famous star of classic big-screen Westerns.

That night, from the window above her kitchen sink, Linda peered into the little room in the back of the house where Matthew kept his computer. In recent months, since the arrival of the virus, Matthew had abandoned his usual habit of watching sports on the flat-screen TV in his front room in favor of sitting at his computer late into the evening, night after night. These days, daylight savings made the days short, the nights long. The computer monitor lit the whole room as if Matthew, and she too, standing there with her hands sunk in cooling dishwater, were peering into a blazing furnace.

You weren't supposed to notice things about your neighbors. You weren't supposed to snoop, to judge. Each to his own. Mind your own business. Good fences. But Linda couldn't resist connecting the dots, recalling those mimeographed handouts from her elementary school days, passed out by an underprepared substitute teacher, or given to the school children when a rare storm rained out recess. She loved the mystery, the puzzle, of what the lines drawn between the numbers in order would create, then the reward of the picture or scene ready to color in. There were always clues, hints: a flash of a tail, the arc of a toothy grin, the slash of a spine. This one would become a galloping horse, this one a whale, that one an owl. Sometimes there were surprises. A creature you couldn't at first imagine. Not a kitten but a dragon. Not a dancer but a snake. This moment, peering from her window into his, felt like that. Your neighbor's business was not yours—until, of course, they became your business and you theirs.

A couple years back, her enterprising daughter had signed her up for Twitter, Facebook, Instagram, and NextDoor Neighbor when Linda's notary public services needed the boost that social media promised. Her social media profiles became essential during lockdown. Under Willow's guidance, Linda learned how to tend them, creating cheerful posts that brought in steady business, a welcome supplement to her part-time paralegal work, monthly child support, and alimony.

Tonight, for the first time, Linda clicked on the "What's Happening" tab on Twitter, then the item right below it: "Capitol Riot." That tab had always been there, on the right, an invitation she had never considered was meant for her. For so long, nothing seemed to be happening—or at least she couldn't see it, especially not online. Now, it seemed, lots was happening. Everywhere. She clicked on "You might like." And after that: "Who to Follow." She felt a bit like Alice in Wonderland, taking a bite of a mushroom and a slice of currant cake, and first sipping, then swigging, from the "Drink Me" bottle.

It didn't take Linda long to find what she was looking for. A few clicks here. A few there. Willow had informed her that Twitter, like social media in general, was intuitive, but until this moment her mother hadn't thought so. But maybe she needed motivation to effectively engage with the intuitive design. Maybe she needed an attempted overthrow of the republic as an incentive to exercise something she had. And suddenly she did.

With a few more clicks, Linda found answers delivered more quickly than television news or the daily regional newspaper flung each morning at her porch. These people, these very busy people on Twitter, they were what's happening. And apparently since the insurrection (as it was now being called), they seldom slept. Citizen journalists, they called themselves, or open-source investigators. Their Twitter handles charmed her: *Belling the Cat. No Nazis for Me Thank You. Deep State Dog.* Linda's Twitter feed, once slow and meandering, populated by real estate listings, local business opportunities, and inspirational memes, became a rush of riot images and video feed. Hours went by. Then days. Linda's new friends—*Did one have friends on Twitter,* she wondered, *or was that only on Facebook? They felt like friends*—were eager to help her answer her daughter's, perhaps everyone's, questions: Who were these people? Where did they come from?

❦

The FBI's online tip form was well organized and surprisingly simple to fill out. Intuitive, you might say. A matter of minutes and it was done. Of course, Linda relied on her own well-organized mental notes and observations, which made it easier. Dates of departure and return. That scruffy "before" beard and long hair. Her Twitter friends had taught her that this was a recommended disguise tactic, not that many felt they would need to hide, victory being so certain. But just in case, a shave and haircut before returning home wouldn't hurt. The scouring of the car. The disappearance of the flag. Then there was his easy-to-find online activity documenting—no, celebrating—Matthew's foray into the Capitol, along with what he called his "regiment," all men from the region, including a former police chief and the son of a prominent real estate developer family. The selfies, the videos. It was all there in red, white, and blue.

As Linda dutifully reviewed the FBI electronic tip form, she recalled those crisp 20s, fresh from the ATM, that Matthew always gave Willow for chicken duty and the special Christmas cookies his mother sent every year. Butter cookies with a whole pecan pressed in the middle. Mrs. Graver always sent two tins, and Matthew walked one over, waiting until she and Willow were home instead of leaving it on the porch. A nice gesture. The cookies were familiar from her youth. The popular recipe could be found on packs of butter that featured what was then called an Indian maiden, kneeling by a blue lake, offering up a tiny facsimile of the very butter package she appeared on. As a child Linda was enchanted by this brand simply because of the young woman with her braids and buckskin dress, the peaceful, pretty landscape and that tiny box in her hands that held an even smaller version of herself holding an even smaller box of butter. Young Linda had even fantasized she might go there one day, somehow walk into that scene, see that lake, those perfect pine trees. Printed inside the waxed interior were recipes you could cut out and save. Recently the newspaper had reported that the Indian maiden was no more, freed from her obedient servitude like Uncle Ben and Aunt Jemima. The waxy package's vista was just the blue lake now, framed by pines reflected on its placid surface, the space where the young woman had knelt for decades empty.

Christmas wasn't that long ago. Their artificial tree still stood in the corner, twinkling. A few cookies waited to be eaten. The tin sat on the kitchen table where Linda worked. A band of carolers decorated its lid, each merry singer depicted with a song sheet and a long knitted scarf, joyfully serenading passersby on a snowy city corner. Willow saved the tins each year, repurposing them. This one, an unusual rectangular shape, she'd already claimed as ideal for her paintbrushes. They had given Matthew their traditional gift: a calendar from the nearby bird sanctuary. The same one hung on their wall. January featured the stately Cooper's hawk, aka chicken hawk, a dapper raptor, not unlike those carolers with a black cap and gray coat, a puffed-out white chest barred with red.

Her review session concluded, Linda clicked the box that declared she was not a robot. She popped open the tin and retrieved a cookie, thick and round, tasting like it always had of butter and sugar and vanilla. Her reward. Perfect. She pressed Send. It was done.

Two weeks later, just after the inauguration, the agents arrived, emerging from a small fleet of black Cadillac Escalades, wearing their black windbreakers proclaiming their identity in yellow block letters on the back: FBI. Official coronavirus masks, KN95, no doubt. *Sedition Hunters* on Twitter used the verb *swarmed* in their tweet. Linda missed the swarm but Willow was there, watching from the vantage point of her second-story bedroom. *Mom,* she texted, *something's going down next door.*

Linda didn't see the text until later. Early that morning she was waiting at the mouth of the canyon in the cul-de-sac where the local family-run assisted living facility was hosting yet another neighbor's dying parent. Olive Grove Guest Home was run by two generations of nurses, assisted by various family members. The old folks' home occupied a special place in the canyon, allowing residents to relocate their aging relatives or themselves as needed. For a notary like Linda, Olive Grove provided steady business.

When the morning's call came through, Linda decided to walk down rather than drive, carrying her attaché case. It was a beautiful morning for a walk. The hills were beginning to green up from the winter rains after the fall's wildfires. The creek was running—low, but running. Two months yet until spring, but she thought she saw the first leaves of wild lilies beginning to unfurl along the road. She hadn't wanted to continue to live in the house where her marriage had failed. That's why they had moved out here, where the sidewalks ended and in the mornings you woke to roosters, and in the afternoons the sound of horses' hooves echoed. Living out here could take the edges off a person. The freeways that took them to school and work were still only twenty minutes away, but the canyon felt like a new old world, a fresh start.

This time it was Karen Vogel's father Ben, a proud man who had apparently intended to live forever and had therefore made no arrangements. Now, before the morphine drip, daughter Karen needed power of attorney drawn up and a do not resuscitate order. Ben was famous in the canyon. The American flag that he daily raised by his home on the main road featured a hand-painted sign attached to the pole's base: *A Pearl Harbor Survivor Lives Here*. Vogel was also known for his birdhouses, handcrafted and personalized to resemble the homes of those who purchased them. The canyon was full of his winsome miniatures, the echo of their owners' homes. Proceeds went to the bird sanctuary. Linda had commissioned one when she and Willow settled in and then, wanting to be friendly, ordered one more because, after all, considering that Matthew's home was the twin of theirs, it would be easy for Mr. Vogel to make two. That was both her first overture to her new neighbor and her first misstep with Matthew, though for the life of her, she couldn't understand what she had done wrong.

"Thanks, but no thanks," Matthew had said from behind his screen door when she and Willow, still toddling, showed up with Vogel's handiwork. The late-afternoon sun slanting through the screen pixelated him.

At first Linda thought Matthew had misunderstood, had imagined she was asking for money. The birdhouses weren't cheap. "It's a gift," she explained. "I had two made. Two for the two identical houses, the two brothers." She pointed to where she had installed hers, suspended from the low-hanging branch of an oak. "This one is our gift to you."

She saw Matthew take a long look at the two of them. She wondered what was going through his mind. Maybe he thought Linda was after something other than money, standing there with her daughter, her arms holding a tiny house. She was still dressed for work, a skirt suit, nylons, heels, the kind of clothes she seldom wore anymore but did back then. She flushed.

"Thanks, but no thanks," Matthew repeated. "Birds don't need handouts and neither do I. And they make their own homes just fine." He closed, just shy of slamming, the door shut.

Linda and her daughter took the short walk back to their home. She told Willow that Matthew was technically right. Birds did indeed make their own homes just fine. And, barring natural disasters, they found their own food as well. Still, Linda wished she had spoken up, reacted differently. She could have pointed out to her neighbor that some birds—say, chickens, free range or not—needed more than they could forage. Such birds needed houses too, coops. Matthew's chickens were certainly well housed. But Linda sensed he was a man who didn't like to be corrected, especially by a woman. And his rejection was too firm. And so the second birdhouse became a dollhouse for Willow.

One day not long after, Karen, Ben's daughter, enlightened her while they waited in line at the post office. The story involved a famous bit of canyon lore regarding the two men's flags and another decal Matthew had earlier removed from his white truck. When he was new to the canyon, his truck's rear window sported an USMC emblem, an eagle straddling a globe pierced by an anchor. Huge. Not subtle. It made an impression.

Karen rolled her eyes. "Vets," she quipped, "gotta love them." But as it turned out, she explained, Matthew was no vet. "Anyone can buy those decals off the internet, you know," Karen said, and that's exactly what Matthew had done. After a few chats with Matthew, Ben Vogel had smelled a rat. "Stolen valor, Pops called it," Karen remembered, describing how he challenged Matthew during one of the volunteer firefighters' regular Wednesday trainings. "I was there," she said. "It was something else. Matthew never came back to the firehouse. So no, Matthew does not want one of Dad's birdhouses. That's the last thing he wants."

Vogel was ninety-five and, until just a few days ago, had been living on his own, raising that flag each morning, filling his bird feeders to attract songbird species, the buffet studded with glossy black sunflower seeds.

From his raised hospital bed, Ben feebly flirted with Linda as she set up the paperwork. "Hey, good lookin', what ya got cookin'?" he quipped with a faint Hank Williams twang, a squinty wink.

"My daughter is the one who cooks," Linda said, smiling behind her mask. "She bakes. All the time. Cakes. Next time I'll bring you a slice."

"I'd like that," Ben said. "I like a good cake." On the rolling tray table in front of him were arranged a plastic cup of water and a plastic plate with a melting popsicle, its wooden stick unmoored from the dissolving orange confection.

She watched as Ben Vogel signed his name for what would be the last time. He didn't need help. A modest signature with some grand flourishes. That "V" leapt. The final "l" stood tall.

"Your dad still has it, doesn't he?" she remarked to Karen as they walked into the living room to finish their business. She gave Karen the canyon discount plus the veteran discount, which meant that all Karen owed her was thanks and a handshake.

"The life force is strong," Karen observed, "until it isn't. Ninety-five!"

❦

"Mom!" Willow called from the kitchen when Linda returned. She was mixing another cake. Italian this time, with olive oil instead of butter. Recipe cut out of the newspaper. Rosemary and almonds and orange zest. A half a dozen eggs. And she had dyed her hair again. When did kids find the time? But time was all they had. The hot pink had been replaced by green, a bright fresh green like those spear-shaped lily leaves poking up from the cold ground. The kitchen smelled of hot citrus and burnt sugar. The calendar was turned to February. A scrub jay preening, gray cape, long blue tail, triumphant with an acorn in its black beak.

The photos on Willow's cell phone told the story. It was a very short story. The agents knew what they were looking for. Matthew had offered no resistance.

"Mom?" Her green-haired daughter looked at her. "You don't seem surprised," Willow said. She wore one of Linda's mother's aprons—green, as it happened, patterned with red apples, the big front pockets edged with white rickrack. What would her own mother have made of the green hair? Or of a neighbor like Matthew, the spectacle of the assault on the Capitol?

"Oh, well, you know, nothing surprises me anymore, Will," Linda said, trying to sound both breezy and world weary. She didn't like to lie to her daughter. This wasn't quite a lie, but it was close. It seemed to work.

"What about his chickens?" Willow asked.

They both looked out the window over the sink to their neighbor's house, the twin of theirs. The little room in the back where Matthew kept his computer was empty. His big white truck was parked in the drive. His flag still hung there, limp on the white flagpole.

Matthew's birds were free-range during the day, strutting their stuff in his fenced yard, pecking at attractive patches of grass and dirt, shimmying their fat feathery behinds down into the earth. But at the end of each day, they needed to be locked up for the night in their secure coop, safe from foxes, bobcats, and the occasional mountain lion on the prowl. Their eggs needed to be collected too, and their water needed replenishing. And their supplemental feed was essential. Who knew when Matthew would be back? He'd left in a hurry, no time to ask for their assistance.

"Well, you know what to do," Linda said. "How to take care of them."

"Without him asking?" Willow seemed skeptical.

"Look," Linda said. "We should help him out. Even if he didn't ask. Sometimes you help people even if they don't ask." *Could it be said that that was what she had done? Helped Matthew?*

"Won't he get mad?" Willow didn't like conflict, especially when it was nearby. She made a face, an exaggerated frown with lots of teeth.

"Don't worry. It's what good neighbors do. And we *are* good neighbors, right?" Linda meant it: they were good neighbors. And so was Matthew. She reminded Willow of the time he'd cut up the fallen oak branch that had blocked their drive, *without asking*. And he had stacked the wood instead of just leaving it.

Willow nodded.

"And think of the chickens, Will." She reached out and touched her daughter's new green hair. She didn't do that so much anymore. Linda could see that Willow was her own person these days. And yet her daughter's green hair felt just like the black. "Plus," Linda paused, tucking some flyaway strands of hair, green as grass, behind her daughter's ear, "we could use the eggs."

The Frontera Grill

A quarter of a century earlier, the upscale Mexican restaurant had arrived in their neighborhood with $10 valet parking and tender green-corn tamales the size of thumbs that cost even more than the parking. Back then, the newly coupled young couple had worried that the end was near. He, Nick, meant the lease on their rent-controlled apartment while she, Maggie, meant their ability to live only five blocks from the Pacific Ocean on community organizer salaries. A proper dinner, with drinks and dessert, would cost half their monthly rent. Nick was opposed on principle. Nick had lots of principles. Principles were cheap, he liked to believe, yet nourishing. Maggie had principles too, but she really would have liked to order from the fancy menu with its artisanal tequilas and exotic ceviches. At least once. But since they could not, they made fun of what they could not and should not afford as they ambled down Fourth Street to pay their bills.

They always paid cash. The utility company offices, that elemental triad of water, electricity, and gas, occupied adjacent corners in the still-quaint downtown, three blocks past the new restaurant and one block from their local bank, into which they faithfully deposited their modest paychecks and withdrew enough currency for bills, saving on everything—the stamps to mail in checks for the bills, the price of the individual checks, the processing charges, the gas to drive downtown instead of walking ten blocks, the quarters for the parking meters if they did drive, the coins for fare if they chose to take the bus. That's how they lived then. They walked around town with cash in their pockets, holding hands, feeling virtuous, solvent, in love. They wore T-shirts from their most recent campaigns like businessmen wore three-piece suits. Thin T-shirts, silkscreened with slogans and demands. Do this. Stop that. Free them. That was, after all, their own business: the business of doing, stopping, and freeing.

Like the swanky restaurant and the utilitarian utility companies, their new apartment complex also stood on Fourth Street. The building bore a suspicious resemblance to the cartoony fake Mission Revival style of a nearby Taco Bell franchise where Nick sometimes succumbed to a 49-cent burrito, principles be damned. The pebbly, pitted stucco of their building reminded Maggie of her acne scars, but they could not afford to be choosy. The nonprofit that managed it promoted affordable housing in the seaside city and had offered them an emergency opening under a civic relocation policy a month after that early morning when a piece of printed yellow cardstock announced that Maggie and Nick and their neighbors had thirty days to find other homes.

Their landlord, famous for his development schemes, had big plans for Bay City Bungalow Court, circa 1948, home to eight aging single-family cottages, big enough for modest postwar family life but not profitable enough for the looming millennium, especially under the city's still-fresh rent-control edicts. Even though it would eventually take him fifteen years to raise the scratch and get all the permits, the landlord wanted everyone out now.

Nick, who had never been evicted before, embraced the yellow notice as a badge of honor. The very forces that he spent his working hours organizing against were now at last oppressing him! Finally. He'd been waiting for them. He safety-pinned the notice to the back of his blue jean jacket, where it seemed to swagger as he walked. He gave impromptu speeches in the courtyard to their neighbors.

But Maggie, whose childhood featured one eviction after another, felt the familiar rise of anxious shame. She feared this meant she'd have to go back, back to where she came from, those bleak suburbs on the other side of the big city, her crazy mother's place, sharing a room with various half- and step-siblings and putting up with whichever short-term stepfather had been installed. She feared this would mean the end of her and Nick. And she had loved the dilapidated charms of their bungalow where, she quietly wailed into his shoulder, as only a twenty-three-year-old could wail, they had fallen in love. This was the best place she had ever lived. Maggie whispered this softly and only to Nick. She sensed his quiet disappointment in her even as he consoled her. They weren't supposed to want things to stay the same. They weren't supposed to be satisfied. They were to expect struggle. Well, yes, what happened to other people would indeed happen to them, starting now.

On day 28, forty-eight desperate hours before the deadline, they made their way to Fourth Street, searching for the address Nick scrawled in ballpoint pen on the back of his hand. They walked and walked, coming closer to the ocean. They climbed the stairs to apartment #12 and, when Nick knocked, the door swung open of its own accord. Perched on the kitchen counter, waiting, her legs crossed and encased in impressive boots, black leather lace-ups with yellow stitching, was Liz. They recognized her from demonstrations and picket lines, from well-intentioned meetings that went on too long, and from her lead vocals in the local all-lesbian rock 'n' roll band. Liz looked like Patty Duke with aviator glasses but sang like Janis Joplin. Once Maggie had watched her belt out "Me and Bobbie McGee" on a rickety rented stage in the Nevada desert to an audience of dusty sunburned do-gooders from around the nation, rebellious, sensibly dressed Catholics and eco-warriors, Grandmothers for Peace, and those stalwarts who showed up for righteous causes anywhere, anytime they could. This time they had gathered at the gates of the Nuclear Test Site, an hour north of Las Vegas, both the middle of nowhere and the middle of everything. Liz pulled everything she could out of the song and then some, changing the pronouns to suit herself. Toward the end, she hopped down into the sand and danced her way across the police line to get arrested with Western Shoshone tribal members while the crowd was still singing along to the endless chorus of "la-da-da-da-das" and "hey hey heys."

Now Liz had landed a real gig and was using her considerable skills set to defend housing access. She wore a suit that seemed at odds with her footwear. She joked that steady employment had cut into her show biz career and civil disobedience activity but had also helped her buy her amazing boots. Doc Martens straight from London, bought locally at the punk shop on Broadway. Liz was, it seemed, their good omen in boots and big glasses. They both knew she didn't have to say yes to them, but she did.

"Solidarity forever," Liz quipped.

Later, walking away with keys in hand and a signed lease, they agreed that Liz was who they wanted to be when they grew up. And that, they believed, would happen any day now. Life was quick, and then long.

The fancy restaurant's remodel retained the original storefront window of the former department store but a stove top with cast-iron comals was installed next to a sliding-glass service window that opened to the sidewalk traffic. A woman was stationed there, patting out fresh tortillas, corn and flour. If lines were long outside, as they often were, fresh flour tortillas smeared with butter and sprinkled with salt were offered. Once, walking downtown on some errand, pausing to check out the scene, Maggie and Nick were mistaken for hungry waiting patrons and given two tortillas, gently folded in thirds, warm in their hands like clean cotton fresh from a clothes dryer. Maggie preferred corn, but this was a delightful treat, the tender pull of the dough when she bit, the sharp sprinkles of salt against the butter. She felt the flat chipped roundness of the browned spots, tasted the iron heat that blackened the edges. That it was free made it even better. Maggie and Nick congratulated themselves as they separated from the prospective diners who, for a moment, they had become somehow, lips all shiny with butter, salt gritty in their mouths before dissolving.

Some fifteen years later, back in town for some good-cause fundraiser, the community they once worked so hard to organize having been sufficiently organized for them to move on to a more disorganized community and, yes, more permanent digs and eventually more profitable employment, Maggie and Nick finally visited the restaurant for the first time.

Why not? They could now afford occasional meals at fancy places like this one. They had graduated from grad school. They had moved inland. They had a mortgage and bills their former selves could not have imagined. Accompanied by their toddler son, they parked their hybrid vehicle across the street at the top of the city parking structure that, despite the era of credit card meters, still accepted quarters and in exchange, if one chose to drive six stories to the top, offered an ocean view. Other landmarks of their past life had been altered or vanished, but the broad blue expanse of the Pacific persevered, fulfilling a cool wet promise on this hot afternoon. Nick lifted their son up so he could see it, but the boy resisted and so they made their way to the stairs. It was the weekend, after lunch and before happy hour, a slow time at even the best restaurants, so Maggie thought they were safe with their kid. He was generally well behaved, oddly sedate, even, the only child of tired older parents, reasoned Maggie even as she worried about his placid nature or what Nick praised as early-onset autonomy and contentment.

They were in luck. The place was deserted. Curbside, a trio of handsome valets in red jackets focused on their cell phones as Maggie and Nick jaywalked across the street, the child between them.

Then they entered the place they had seen only from the sidewalk and in the pages of newspapers and lifestyle magazines. The walls were like giant chalkboards, painted an ashy black and etched with glowing neon line drawings of elegant people and fanciful creatures that seemed to light the cool dark room. Music played, familiar American rock 'n' roll but crooned in Spanish. A woman stood at the comals, stacking tortillas. Maggie wondered if she could be the same woman, if people stayed so long at that kind of job. The woman offered a tortilla to their son even though there was no wait. The child was always being offered gifts like this. Cookies at the bakery, strawberries and apple wedges at the farmers' market, once a Christmas tree ornament from a thrift store clerk who appreciated his good behavior. That constant of his childhood surprised Maggie. Her own had not been marked by anonymous spontaneous generosity, not at all, even though she imagined her child self had been as well behaved as her son. Maggie hoped that the boy would see the world differently because it was always smiling at him, offering itself for free, like this tortilla. She hoped it would help him open up, smile back, give back.

"Su hijo es muy guapo," the woman said.

"Gracias," Maggie answered.

With three quick bites, the boy chewed the tortilla into a face mask as he liked to do at home. Tilting his face upward, he donned it with exaggerated ceremonial care, spreading it across his forehead and the round rise of his fat cheeks, and marched after the hostess to their table. On top of the white cloth, a basket of chips waited next to a glowing candle. Maggie pushed the basket toward him. He settled in, the thin tortilla remaining adhered to his face, while they examined the menu and placed their orders.

Her son consumed the chips as Maggie knew he would—one chip, then another, then another, slowly, rhythmically, attentive to nibbling each crisp triangle in exactly the same manner of satisfaction. The fanciful décor entranced him, must have seemed like his own wild crayoned drawings, and he remained docile throughout the meal, the tortilla mask balanced on his upturned face, the chips steadily disappearing through its gnawed mouth hole. When he finally emptied the basket, the boy, still wearing his tortilla mask, now a glistening limp round, deserted their table. He climbed down from the booster seat and walked to the vacant neighboring table, cloaked like all the tables by a long, nearly floor-length white tablecloth. He picked up the edge of the cloth, peered under, and then disappeared beneath just as their waitress arrived with a new basket of chips.

By then Nick and Maggie had each had a giant margarita, the type they had scoffed at for years, but that they now had to admit were pretty damn good. Worth the wait, Maggie quipped. A cucumber jalapeno margarita for her, a Cadillac with blue agave nectar for him, served in a heavy Mexican glass trimmed with cobalt blue. They watched their child's actions with the quiet delight of slightly drunk parents.

Their waitress found the child's relocation charming. She slid a full basket of chips halfway under the table and waited until the boy pulled it the rest of the way. She replaced their empty glasses with two more drinks. Maggie finished her pescado veracruzano with fennel. She resisted picking up the plate to tilt the juices into her mouth, but she surely thought about it. Nick sopped up what was left of his mole sauce with the remaining tortillas. They divided what was left of the boy's abandoned portobello mushroom quesadilla. They talked about who they had been when they last lived here and spoke about who they were now. Maggie hoped they were still the same. Nick wasn't sure. Then dessert arrived, a slice of tres leches cake and a goat cheese–honey-jalapeno flan plus a concoction the waitress called an espresso martini, and Maggie remembered their son was missing out. They had, after all, ordered the cake for him. With the exception of tortilla chips, the child was eating only white food these days. Flour tortillas. White rice. White bread. Rice noodles. Peeled bananas. Saltines. Yogurt. Sometimes all at once, on a white plate.

Maggie approached the neighboring table with a spoonful of the creamy cake. A quick peek under the tablecloth revealed that the boy was not where she'd thought he was. The sense of imminent calamity that had arrived with the birth of the child was there—ready, waiting. She felt like she must swallow something she had not yet eaten. But she knew he couldn't have gotten far. She began to inspect the nearby tables, proceeding in a hunched manner to lift each tablecloth, finally resorting to a full-out crawl because that felt best and was, she believed, less noticeable. She was wearing jeans, after all. And the room was dark, even in the afternoon. Plus the margaritas and dessert martini had left her feeling playful, so her judgment was understandable. Or so she believed. Besides, there was no one there to notice. She was trying not to worry, but she was beginning to. Then she saw a tiny shoe sticking out from under a table near the large picture window up front.

Those were the showcase tables, visible from the street, where years earlier, celebrities chowed down on seafood pozole and carne asada and chile verde. Once, on their way to pay an overdue telephone bill, Maggie and Nick glimpsed the pretty-boy rock star with good politics who they had been arrested with. He'd recognized them, certainly not by name but by that kind of familiar awareness one acquires through the years after proximity at picket lines and marches and sit-ins and in LAPD holding tanks. You didn't know everybody but at the same time you did. You had been through something together. You'd shown up for the same events, time and time again. The rock star lifted his chin and nodded. His suntanned cheekbones were high and sharp, like the Malibu ridgeline shadowed at sunset. His hair, parted on the side, still long, still silky, moved like a slow wave breaking on a sunny day at Zuma. His tresses—Maggie thought there was no other word for them—seemed to encapsulate a certain 1970s Southern California, Maggie's teenage years from eighth grade to community college, from Girl Scouts to assorted Third World liberation fronts. Maggie looked at his plate. Pescado veracruzano.

Now, she scrambled over to where her son hid, trying not to disturb the new customers settling into the adjacent table, a dapper middle-aged man and two young girls, identical twins, both in old-school party dresses. Beautiful girls, beautiful dresses, the kind that girls used to wear on very special occasions, Easter or someone's wedding. White Peter Pan collars, smocked bodices, bows in the back tied with merry expertise. The girls were both black-haired, of Asian descent, as people say. There was something vaguely familiar about the man, who was white and balding and wore glasses, but this was, after all, the city where they had lived and worked for many years and so there was something vaguely familiar about almost everyone in town, whether Maggie knew them or not. This man probably lived north of Montana, as locals called it, that street named for the state on the Canadian border that in this town marked the boundary between those doing well enough and those doing much, much better.

Maggie felt the man's eyes on her. She imagined what she looked like, a woman of a certain age who didn't hide it, scrambling around on the floor holding aloft a spoonful of white cake. She hoped to elicit amusement, some kind of shared parental empathy, but sensed mild disgust instead. His attention did not linger. He was focused on the vast menu open before him, was already interrogating the waitress in a raised voice about a dish that used to be on the menu but was no longer there and couldn't he order that? His daughters—she presumed they were his daughters by how they spoke to him—along with the waitress (their waitress, the very same tolerant, helpful waitress), were offering alternatives—"Tiger shrimp enchiladas in green sauce? Mushroom mulitas? Crab tostada Ensenada?"—but the man was having none of it.

"Come out," she whispered to her son.

The boy stayed put. His sturdy shoe disappeared under the table.

Maggie lifted the tablecloth and peered inside. There he was, looking so pleased with himself, so delighted, sitting cross-legged with his very own basket of half-eaten tortilla chips. The tortilla mask was wadded in his fist. He *was* a handsome boy, as the woman had said, even with cold butter coating his face like greasy sweat. He didn't look like her, brown and small, the kind of person some people sometimes spoke Spanish to. He looked like Nick, which maybe, she thought, accounted for all the smiles, all the freebies given to a blond boy with a bowl cut and a fat-cheeked face.

"Come in," he said. "It's nice." He patted the empty place beside him. It was a table for two, on top and below.

"I can't," she said.

His disappointment was palpable. His brown eyes, which had been bright a moment earlier, darkened. That silent child self she worried about swiftly returned. She felt him withdrawing further under the table. He didn't often extend invitations. He had words, but seldom used them. He had no friends at the child care center where he spent his days, no friends in the neighborhood. At home he was happiest by himself, content to play alone behind a closed door. He seldom asked for anything. Perhaps, the pediatrician had suggested gently, because his parents anticipated his needs too well. Maggie hoped the doctor was right.

"Come in," he repeated. "Just for a minute. Please." The words carried a demand, but there was none in that small voice. There was just effort. A great effort.

"Okay," she said, giving in. "Just for a minute." Maggie lifted the tablecloth and crawled under the canopy formed by the table and cloth, using her knees and one hand, the other hand still grasping the dessert spoon. She arranged herself with care, finding enough room, more than she imagined. All she had to do was bow her head slightly. She sat there with her son, observing what gave him pleasure. A calm shelter. The tablecloth tent seemingly emitting its own white light. His very own basket of chips. The clean, cool floor tiles like spaces on a giant game board. His mother beside him, doing as he instructed, albeit awkwardly in her short stout body. It was cozy, Maggie thought. It was safe. It was, she thought, a sit-in of sorts, like in the old days. At first you feel vulnerable, silly, embarrassed, sitting down while the rest of the world remains standing. You see their feet, boots and shoes. You see the dirt others cannot. You are small again. Then, Maggie remembered, you become rooted, somehow stronger together. Then they drag you away. This was a few minutes of their life together. She would remember. Her son would not.

She handed him the spoon with the scoop of snowy white cake still miraculously intact. "Try this," she said.

He cleaned the spoon with one smooth swallow and smiled with rare approval. "Try this," he said, matching her inflection. "You eat now." He very formally handed her his tortilla mask. It had been squeezed tightly, with the special ferocity of a child's fist.

He waited to see what she would do.

Maggie took it, unrolled it, and held it up, a thin handkerchief of dough, marbled with lard, freckled by heat, features bitten into it by her son's teeth. It was easy to resist the gentle urge to drape it on her face though she held it up close and made him laugh as she winked through his eye holes. Then she rolled it and chewed it obediently. She did what a mother does: what her child wanted. It wasn't as good as the one she remembered from years earlier, but it wasn't too bad either. And free.

As she swallowed, she heard the man's voice at the next table, still arguing with the waitress, getting louder. His rising whine reminded her of a troubling sound her car had made once that caused an expense they could not afford. Then Maggie realized.

He was an actor. Of course he was. There were so many in this town. They had encountered actors often enough when they'd lived here. This man was the lead actor in a hit cable TV series. He played a man just like this one at the table—perpetually, petulantly, pugilistically disappointed by those around him. His character's name in the series was the same as the actor's real name. Nick didn't like the show, thought it was funny but also cruel, too cruel. This was, she thought, exactly like a scene in an episode of his own show! The disappointing menu. The unhelpful waitress. The disloyal daughters siding with the useless waitress. The crazy customer crawling around the floor holding a spoon and taking up residence under the table next to him. The actor would never get what he wanted. The world would never give it to him. He began to shout, just like his character on the show. From where she sat, the white tablecloth like a half-raised theater curtain, Maggie could see the lower half of each of his trousered legs and his expensive iconic black-and-white sneakers. The rubber white toe caps gleamed as if polished. He began to stamp his feet.

Later Maggie couldn't quite remember how she got out from under that table with her young son and walked back across the restaurant, how their playful hide-and-seek sit-in ended. She must have emerged, gotten to her feet, straightened her jeans and shirt, pulled her son after her, walked past the actor, the two well-dressed girls, the put-upon waitress and the sadistic comic scene unfolding at the showcase window table. She and Nick and their son must have paid their bill, leaving an excellent tip for their waitress to make up for the one she would not be receiving from the disappointed actor.

All three walked to the fundraiser after that, down that very familiar sidewalk that Maggie and Nick had once walked back and forth, back and forth, but this time they tugged their child between them. Later that evening, after all the speeches and testimonials, they no doubt wrote a sizeable check to yet another not-quite-lost cause. Liz should have been there, Maggie remembered thinking. Liz should have been the director of this organization, giving the keynote.

On the way home, they detoured to drive past their old apartment building, pointing it out to their still awake, although barely, son. "We used to live there," Maggie told him. "Before you were born. Many years ago. See? It looks like a Taco Bell."

That child, their son, is a teenager now, an actor himself, taking auditions in the city where they used to live. He's just fine. He uses all his words now, all the time, and other people's words too. The world still smiles at him. He still gets things for free. He is, his mother believes, happy, generous, grateful for what is given. Not like that other actor.

Liz, who had greeted them so warmly at their new apartment and given them the keys to their new life, as she called it, bought a round-trip ticket to England one December not long after that afternoon in apartment #12. Liz had always wanted to go to London and, as she told them, now that she had the money, thanks to her new job, she would. She'd wear her new boots too, those lace-up Doc Martens Maggie so admired. She wanted to show the boots, Liz jested, where they had come from. Ha, ha, ha. On December 21, the winter solstice, Liz flew back home on Pan Am flight 103, which exploded over Lockerbie, Scotland.

❦

The fancy restaurant is closing now, after twenty-five years. Maggie heard it on the radio. Its two famous female chefs are moving on. Long ago one had been married to the architect who designed the restaurant. They divorced, and today she is married to a woman. You can do that now. Her ex-husband, the architect, eventually married the other chef, her friend. They are nudists, with children about the age of Maggie and Nick's son. Maggie read all about it in the *LA Times*. Yet their lives can't be as simple as the newspaper described, Maggie thinks, because nothing is.

Maggie also read that the dissatisfied actor divorced his wife. She wonders about the two girls with their black hair, which parent they live with or if custody is shared. She supposes she could look it up. You can look up almost anything these days. For example, their former landlord died before his development plans were realized. Today, the site of the Bay City Bungalow Court remains a vacant lot circled by a cyclone fence, growing tumbleweeds with no place to roll. Unbelievable. His heirs are enmeshed, as they say, in a court struggle. Enmeshed!

For another example of what you can learn online, their friend Liz had been seated in seat 39C. The plane was the *Clipper Maid of the Seas*, a lyrical if unlikely name for an aircraft. Liz had been all of thirty years old, which seems so, so young now that Maggie and Nick are poised to cross that borderline between middle age and old age on demographic surveys, the ones that leave only one further box to check. Another example: Doc Martens, Liz's cherished boots, are no longer made in England but instead manufactured in China and Thailand in sweatshops.

Sometimes Maggie wonders if the famous actor was ever asked if the girls were his real daughters. She used to get that question about her son all the time. Now people just ask if she is his grandmother. She understands why. She is as old as some grandmothers out there. She and Nick are still together. They grew up and, as they planned, became like Liz. Do-gooders. It was, she thinks sometimes, the least they could do. They owed it to Liz, who gave them what they needed, when they needed it and made, Maggie fiercely believes, their life together possible.

Acknowledgments

Thanks to the journals in which versions of some of these stories first appeared. "False Flag" was published in *Citric Acid*. "Everyone Was Singing 'Freiheit'" appeared in *Air/Light*. "The Frontera Grill," "The Mayor and the Folksinger," and "Ocean Park #12" were published in the *Santa Monica Review*. "A Pretty Penny" appeared in *Faultline*. "Cielito Lindo" was published in *Green Mountains Review* and also appeared in *Sudden Fiction Latino: Short-Short Stories from the United States and Latin America*.

Thanks to Andrea Bowers for the use of her artwork for the cover, a much-appreciated gesture of support and solidarity.

Many thanks to the team at the University of Nevada Press and the editors of the New Oeste series, especially Daniel Olivas.

I have been fortunate in my teachers and remain grateful: the late Oakley Hall and Don Heiney of the Programs in Writing at UC Irvine along with CSULB's Rafael Zepeda, SMC's Jim Krusoe, and especially Richard Bausch who, for a few pandemic years, gave me a place back at the workshop table at Chapman University where so many of these stories were born.

Gratitude and respect to my sisters and their daughters, and to my extended family, and my scruffy and political pals who have been another kind of family. And abiding thanks to my lifelong communities: my faithful colleagues and students at Irvine Valley College, the little college in the orange groves, and those of my summer life, the brilliant and generous poets and writers at the Community of Writers in Olympic Valley, especially Brett Hall Jones and Louis B. Jones.

I owe so much to friends and fellow writers, people who kept asking after my writing and, in doing so, kept me writing: Carolyn Allport, Roy Bauer, Dawn Bonker, Diana Burbano, Mary Camarillo, Wayne Clayton, Sarah Rafael García, Donna Hilbert, Anne Holmes, Petra Kolle, Peter Lefèvre, Mari L'Esperance, Mary Mason, Yxta Maya Murray, Emanuele Romussi, Virginia Shank, Sally Shore, Linda Thomas, Maw Shein Win, Mitsuye Yamada, Hilary Zaid, and Mary Zaragoza. Gratitude to Michael Jaime Bercerra and Dagoberto Gilb for showing me how it was done.

Special thanks to my friends from my first years in Irvine: Greg and Jeff Bills-Solomon, Vicki Forman, and Rhoda Huffey, and from my years in SMC's 30B workshop: Janice Shapiro and Monona Wali.

Thank you, Michelle Latiolais, for your faith in me and in these stories and for keeping your promise to Oakley.

And to Andrew Tonkovich and L Alvarez Tonkovich, so often my first readers and always the two loves of my life.

About the Author

Lisa Alvarez, born and raised in Los Angeles, has worked with many peace, justice, and civil rights campaigns. She earned an MFA in writing at UC Irvine. She is a professor of English at Irvine Valley College and codirects the summer writer's workshops at the Community of Writers in Olympic Valley, California. Her work has appeared in *Air/Light, Anacapa Review, Citric Acid, Faultline, Huizache, Santa Monica Review,* among other publications. She lives in Modjeska Canyon.